DATING A COWGIRL

CALLAHANS OF COPPER CREEK BOOK 5

NATALIE DEAN

DEDICATION

I'd like to dedicate this book to YOU! All of my wonderful readers that have been following my stories over the years.

We're embarking on another new journey through Copper Creek. I hope you enjoy these stories as much as you've loved the Baker brothers!

Thank you to my biggest fans.... There's a lot of you! Jess, Bernie, Wren, Judy, Sherry, Vicci, Phyllis, Debbie, Indra, Jennifer, Carol, Jeanette, Margaret, Paul, and I know there's more I didn't list. But thank you all!

And I can't leave out my wonderful mother, son, sister, and Auntie. I love you all, and thank you for helping me make this happen.

Most of all, I thank God for blessing me on this endeavor.

~

AND... I've got a special team of advance readers who are always so helpful in pointing out any last minute corrections that need to be made. I'm so thankful to those of you who are so helpful!

ALSO BY NATALIE DEAN

CONTEMPORARY ROMANCE

Copper Creek Romances

BAKER BROTHERS OF COPPER CREEK
Copper Creek Romances Series 1

Cowboys & Protective Ways

Cowboys & Crushes

Cowboys & Christmas Kisses

Cowboys & Broken Hearts

Cowboys & Second Chances

Cowboys & Wedding Woes

Cowboys' Mom Finds Love

CALLAHANS OF COPPER CREEK
Copper Creek Romances Series 2

Making a Cowgirl

Marrying a Cowgirl

Christmas with a Cowgirl

Trusting a Cowgirl

Dating a Cowgirl

Catching a Cowgirl

Loving a Cowgirl

Marrying a Cowboy

KEAGANS OF COPPER CREEK

Copper Creek Romances Series 3

Some Cowboys are Off-Limits

Some Cowgirls Love Single Dads

Some Cowboys are Infuriating

Some Cowboys Don't Like City Girls

Some Cowboys Heal Broken Hearts

Some Cowgirls are Worth Protecting

Some Cowboys are Just Friends

Some Cowboys Fall for Hidden Stars

Some Cowboys Come Home for Christmas

Some Cowboys Brave the Flames

Some Cowboys Fight for Love

PALMERS OF COPPER CREEK

Copper Creek Romances Series 4

Mateo & Nicole

Sophia & Cameron

Roman & Olivia

Camilla & Dallas

Isabelle & Jason

Marcus & Wynter

Miller Family Saga

BROTHERS OF MILLER RANCH

Miller Family Saga Series 1

Her Second Chance Cowboy

Saving Her Cowboy

Her Rival Cowboy

Her Fake-Fiance Cowboy Protector

Taming Her Cowboy Billionaire

BROTHERS OF MILLER RANCH SERIES BUNDLE

MILLER BROTHERS OF TEXAS

Miller Family Saga Series 2

The New Cowboy at Miller Ranch

Humbling Her Cowboy

In Debt to the Cowboy

The Cowboy Falls for the Veterinarian

Almost Fired by the Cowboy

Faking a Date with Her Cowboy Boss

MILLER BROTHERS OF TEXAS SERIES BUNDLE

BRIDES OF MILLER RANCH, N.M.

Miller Family Saga Series 3

Cowgirl Fallin' for the Single Dad

Cowgirl Fallin' for the Ranch Hand

Cowgirl Fallin' for the Neighbor

Cowgirl Fallin' for the Miller Brother

Cowgirl Fallin' for Her Best Friend's Brother

Cowboy Fallin' in Love Again

BRIDES OF MILLER RANCH, N.M. SERIES BUNDLE

~

Though I try to keep this list updated in each book, you may also visit my website nataliedeanbooks.com for the most up to date information on my book list.

CONTENTS

Chapter 1	1
Chapter 2	10
Chapter 3	20
Chapter 4	29
Chapter 5	37
Chapter 6	46
Chapter 7	55
Chapter 8	65
Chapter 9	74
Chapter 10	83
Chapter 11	92
Chapter 12	101
Chapter 13	110
Chapter 14	120
Chapter 15	129
Chapter 16	139
Chapter 17	148
Chapter 18	156
Chapter 19	165
Chapter 20	175
Chapter 21	184
Chapter 22	193
Chapter 23	202
Chapter 24	212
Chapter 25	220
Chapter 26	228
Chapter 27	235
Chapter 28	238
Chapter 29	243
Chapter 30	247
Epilogue	250

$$1$$

____

Faye

Faye collided with the reception counter. Her elbows rested against the laminate countertop and she put on her prettiest smile as she looked up at Adam Cullen. As far as mechanics go, he probably had to be the cutest one she'd ever met.

He was built like a cowboy, but she'd never seen him on a horse. There was grease under his nails and smudged across his cheekbone. She'd always been a sucker for a guy who had a good work ethic.

Adam glanced up at her from the computer in front of him. His smile matched hers before he glanced in the direction where her sister and future brother-in-law waited. "You guys make your decision on that truck?"

She shifted and tilted her head. "Riley said he'd pay for the parts as long as I pay for the labor."

He glanced once more over to Grace and Riley, confusion marring his handsome face. "Isn't Riley dating your sister?"

"Engaged, actually."

"But you're the one keeping the truck."

Faye nodded. "Grace said it's too much work."

Adam chuckled, and the sound of it slid down her spine like a trickle of warm water, giving her all kinds of goosebumps. "You have no idea. Well, if you're intent on putting in a new engine and rebuilding the transmission, the labor is going to be—"

"Actually…"

He stopped typing and glanced at her again. "You *don't* want me to fix your truck?"

She fidgeted beneath his stare. When she'd come over here, she'd been full of excitement. The rush of knowing Riley would help get her truck fixed had probably given her more confidence than she should have had.

Adam was a *real* mechanic. What made her think that she could convince him to offer his services for free? Now that she thought about it, she knew she couldn't ask such a thing. Faye squirmed some more then nibbled on her lower lip. This would be different if they were friends. The more she dwelled on it, the more she realized her mistake.

Faye cleared her throat and mumbled, "Yes. I want you to fix it."

"Okay, I can put you on the schedule—"

"But I don't think I can afford your rates."

Once again, Adam stilled. He stared at her like she'd grown another head, and she might as well have. Who in their right mind would ask a guy to fix her truck for nothing? The worst part was that she barely had any money, and she definitely didn't have enough to pay for even a percentage of what it would probably cost.

Faye peeked at him and gave him a lopsided smile. "I don't suppose I could help out. Would you let me assist you or anything?"

He twisted away from the computer and rested his elbow on the counter. "You want me to build your transmission and replace your engine for free?"

"With my help..." she murmured. Her face flushed hotter than it ever had. Yep, this wasn't going at all how she'd viewed it in her head. She fidgeted, pulling away from the counter.

If only he'd give her some kind of smile to show her that she wasn't absolutely crazy. But that didn't seem likely at all. Nothing could make this moment any worse. He needed to just tell her that he wasn't able to do such a thing and leave it at that.

Faye couldn't help it. She beat him to it. "I'm sorry. I shouldn't have even asked. You know what? Don't put me on that schedule after all. We can sell the darn thing." Before he could make some snide comment about there being no way she'd get anything for that truck in the first place, she charged for the door. She didn't even bother explaining to her sister or Riley what had just occurred.

All she could do was send a prayer heavenward that Adam didn't breathe a word of this conversation to anyone. The last thing she wanted was for people in town to talk about how airheaded and entitled she was.

She was a fool; that much was clear. What did she expect? It wasn't like she'd been thinking he'd do any of it without some kind of quid pro quo. The only problem was that she had nothing to offer.

Absolutely nothing.

By the time Grace and Riley made it out to the truck, Faye had slipped and shrunk into the smallest size possible in the back seat. She covered her searing cheeks with her hands, but there was no hiding just how embarrassed she was. Hopefully, neither one of them would ask what happened.

Faye groaned. Inwardly, she prayed Adam hadn't said anything.

Riley and Grace stood outside of the driver's side door and chatted. Their voices were muffled, but they didn't sound like they were worried about what had just happened. They didn't sound amused either. Maybe fate would smile down on her and she wouldn't have to talk about it with Grace at all.

Her younger sister opened the door and climbed in. The truck shifted when she shut the door. Grace didn't turn around right away. She seemed more intent on watching her fiancé get on his motorcycle and drive away. Why wasn't she putting her key into the ignition?

The second he got on the main road, Grace met Faye's gaze through the rearview mirror. Faye couldn't tell if her sister was smiling or if she was waiting for something specific. That was the problem with the small rectangular reflective device.

"Well?" Grace asked.

"Well, what?"

"Are you going to tell me why you ran out of there like your hair was on fire?"

Faye shrunk back deeper into the seat. "I'm upset."

"Because?"

She let out a heavy sigh before turning toward the window. Emotion burned behind her eyes and threatened to come up the back of her throat. Crying right now would only make the situation ten times worse. She should have known better than to think she could do anything to save her mom's truck. It was like all of her sisters and even her father were moving on. She was the only one who was willing to cling to the vague memories she had of her mother.

One solitary tear slipped down her cheek in a hot, unforgiving streak. She brushed at it with the heel of her palm. "I don't want to get rid of the truck."

"Yeah. I got that."

"Well, did you also realize that I can't exactly pay for the labor?"

"Faye—"

"No. You don't get it. Like you said before we came. You don't even remember mom. Well, I do. And this truck is the only thing that I have to remember her by."

"We have pictures, home videos—"

"Never mind. You don't get it. That's fine. Just—can we go home now?"

"So what? You're just going to give up like that? Riley offered to pay for the parts. That's like half the battle."

"Yeah. I get it. He's a saint, and I should be grateful that he was willing to help out. But it doesn't do me a lick of good if I can't find someone who is willing to help me fix the truck in the first place."

Her sister grew silent. There, she finally got the whole picture. Faye lost this round. The truck would have to be sold, but at least they'd each get a small cut—whatever that might be. "What's a truck worth these days? You know, the ones that are sold for parts?"

"Faye..."

There was that voice again. The pitying one that Grace could use so easily. "Just don't, okay? I thought there would be a way. Clearly, there isn't one. So I'm going to do some research and find out what we can get for it."

Faye crossed her arms and glared out the window toward the mechanic's shop. There was only one good thing about this failure she could see. At least no one else had been there to observe her falling flat on her face. Not Adam's father. Not the secretary. Not even Bridget.

That was something.

Grace started the truck, but her soft voice still managed to rise over the sound of the engine. "Maybe dad will—"

Faye groaned. "I said drop it. Besides, you and I both know that dad doesn't want anything to do with this truck. He's said as much himself when you had to take it in to get it fixed the first time."

"I guess you're right."

"My only shot at being able to get it fixed is finding someone who is willing to do some charity work for me. I mean, I was even willing to help, you know? He didn't have to be so mean about it."

A quiet gasp escaped Grace's lips, but it might as well have been as loud as a lion's roar for how it made Faye feel.

She jumped and swung her gaze to meet Grace's through the mirror. "What?" Faye asked.

"You didn't ask him to fix this pro bono, did you?"

And just like that, the blush returned with a vengeance. Why did Faye have to be such a blabber mouth? Grace had finally allowed them to drop the subject, and then Faye had to go and spill all the embarrassing beans where her sister could see every single one with absolute clarity.

"*Faye*. Please tell me you didn't. Dad raised us better than that. We don't ask for handouts. You should have—"

"Save it. I know. Don't you think I thought of that? I should have figured out a way to get it fixed on my own, but that's sorta hard when I'm always stuck on the ranch doing all the work that my sisters used to do." She let the words spew forth from her mouth, not caring if they caused Grace any discomfort.

Yes, it wasn't Grace's fault that she'd found a job she loved and she could help people work through hard stuff. But out of the seven of them, there were less than half still carrying the weight of the family business.

Her father could hire as many men as he wanted, but just as Faye remained connected to her mother, she felt the same pull to her father. She could see how it tore him up inside to have all her sisters leaving the nest and finding men of their own.

Well, that wasn't going to be her. Faye was loyal. She'd remain by his side until the end if that's what he wanted.

It was just too bad she couldn't bring herself to ask for his help with the truck. No one understood. Not even her father. She was completely alone.

Faye could feel Grace's eyes on her through that blasted mirror, but she refused to meet her sister's gaze. There would be no talking about this. There would be no hashing it out. She'd finally come to the most logical explanation and that was fine.

Perfectly fine.

She needed to get her thoughts off the truck and onto something else—anything else. Thinking about the truck would only serve to make her day that much worse.

Dumb truck.

Dumb Riley for being willing to help.

And dumb Adam for making a bad situation ten times worse.

Adam was a few years older, so she hadn't interacted with him much when they were younger. She'd never really been curious about him until this exact moment. Hadn't he left town? Was it for a job? Or maybe it was for college. She couldn't remember, and the town's gossips didn't seem to have much to say about him anyway.

He was the kind of guy a girl could fantasize about, which

was probably the reason she was so willing to allow her thoughts to linger.

Adam was quiet, but he had kind eyes. She loved the way they wrinkled as if he'd spent every waking moment smiling.

Though she knew for sure that was one thing that wasn't accurate. The way he'd looked at her so dumbfounded at her request made it perfectly clear that Adam was capable of making other expressions as well—grumpy ones, to be exact.

So why was she suddenly wishing she could turn this truck around and go demand that he make an offer on what he was willing to do?

The truck.

All of her motives had more to do with the truck and less with the person who might be able to fix it. The image of his beautiful face was trespassing in her head at the moment, and she wanted him out.

Except for some reason she couldn't make that happen. Adam had set up shop in her mind and he had no intention of leaving.

Wait a minute.

Did that mean that he might be a clue to something she hadn't seen for herself? It was possible he might have been willing to fix her truck. Had she left too early to make that miracle happen?

Well, it was too late now. They were already halfway home. If she wanted to go talk to Adam about fixing her truck, she'd have to do it another time.

There was only one problem. Her heart didn't want to be patient. That little organ had a mind of its own and wanted to turn this truck around right away. But one look at her sister, and she knew better than to ask for it.

Faye leaned forward, scooting closer to the edge of her seat. "Can I ask a favor?"

Grace shot a look at her over her shoulder. "Okay."

"Can I take the truck around? After we get home, of course."

"Why?"

Faye flinched. Yep. Her sister couldn't just let her have this —no questions asked. "Do I really have to answer that?"

"It's my—"

"No, it's not."

"You didn't even know what I was going to say."

Faye scooted back, rolling her eyes. "Really? You were going to say this is your truck. But the way I see it, it's gonna be mine until I find someone who is willing to buy it."

There it was. The look of resignation. Man, her sister didn't have the fight in her that she used to. That worked out better for Faye than it did for anyone else.

2

Adam

A pair of dirty sneakers entered Adam's vision from where he was beneath a car that had been brought in right after the Callahans left. He turned his head then got back to work on the oil change. "You all done with Keagan's truck?"

Bridget huffed. Her feet shifted before her tilted face appeared. "That piece of junk? I did what I could, but I'm not a miracle worker. Why do all the cowboys around here have problems with their cars?"

His lips quirked into a smile. "Because everyone who lives in Copper Creek is pretty much a cowboy."

"You know what I mean." She settled onto the concrete, crossing her legs. "What did the Callahans want this time? Are they finally willing to accept that their truck is on its last leg?"

A grunt escaped his lips as he worked his magic. "I told

them the same thing you've been telling them. It needs a complete overhaul if they want to keep it running."

"That doesn't answer my question."

He glanced at her. "Grace seems ready to let go of the truck, but not her sister."

"Faye?" Bridget let out a chuckle. "Of course not. That girl will never get rid of that truck."

Adam edged out from under the car and pulled himself into a seated position. He pulled a dirty rag from his pocket and wiped his hands on it. "Why is that?"

"Because that truck belonged to her mother."

Shoving the rag back into his pocket, Adam got to his feet. "I'm sure if Faye's mother was willing to part with it, Faye can do the same. It's not worth much as it is." He brushed past Bridget, who had stood up with him, and he headed for the office so he could print up the invoice.

Soft, padded footsteps followed him. Bridget was usually really good about getting right to work when she came into the shop. It wasn't a surprise his father had hired her on the spot. But she could be a little chatty.

He placed his hand on the computer mouse and moved it around until the screen brightened. Bridget leaned her back against the counter, her arms folded and her gaze on him.

All it took was one glance in her direction for her to continue the conversation they had apparently not completed. "I thought you said you grew up here."

"Yeah. So?"

Her brows creased. "How can you be so obtuse?"

Adam's hand stilled. "What are you talking about?"

"Their mother died when they were young, remember?"

His heart sank. Bridget was right. How could he have forgotten something so important? Granted, the girls never really left the ranch. They didn't talk about their mother, and the people in town never really brought it up that he could recall. But now that Bridget had mentioned it, he didn't have any problems remembering.

"I would bet you anything that Faye is broken up about this whole thing."

"Yeah," he murmured.

"Did she say anything?"

He peeked at Bridget for a moment. "She said that Riley would pay for the parts."

Bridget's brows lifted. "Man, that guy has a heart of gold."

She was right about that, too. If he'd been paying attention, Adam might have realized that Faye wasn't trying to get a handout. She was desperately clinging to a memory of her mother. And while he allowed his thoughts to spiral into a place he wasn't prepared to visit, Bridget started talking about something else.

Maybe he should call the Callahans and see if there was a possibility of a payment arrangement. Or he could talk to his dad about lowering the cost of labor. From what he knew, the Callahans were well off enough it would only take one phone call to Zeke to get this job paid for.

But then why hadn't Faye done that when she was here?

"What about you? Anything fun this weekend?"

Adam jumped and stared at Bridget. "What?"

"There's a rodeo this weekend. Didn't you say you wanted to learn how to do that sort of thing?" The smile she wore mocked him. He could tell just by looking at her that Bridget thought the idea of Adam riding a horse at the rodeo was hilarious.

"You know well enough that I don't know how to ride."

Bridget snickered. "That's the best part of this whole thing. You don't know how to ride but you grew up here. How could you live your entire life in a rancher's town and never go riding?"

"It wasn't for lack of trying," he scoffed, "Most of my friends lived in town."

Understanding filled her expression. "You were a townie."

"You were a city girl. I don't see why that matters."

Her smile returned. "Hey, isn't that girl you like in the rodeo?" Bridget snapped her fingers a few times. "I can't remember her name. What is it? Rose? Daisy? It's a flower name, right?"

"Dahlia," he muttered. "And it's none of your business. Speaking of which, don't you have some work to get to?"

Bridget frowned. "You're no fun."

"This is a place of business, not a gossip hub. Go find something to do, will you?"

She huffed but started toward the shop. Her footsteps slowed and it took everything in his power not to let out a groan. Her soft voice was the only thing that stopped him. "You know what I would do?"

"You'll have to elaborate." Adam kept his focus trained on the computer, but his ears were burning.

"About Dahlia. You wanna know what I would do?"

"I don't suppose you're going to give me a choice to listen or not."

"Nope. What I would do is find some common ground. She's a rodeo star. Learn how to ride a horse or compete in a show that's coming up. They have amateur events too, you know."

Adam sighed and faced her. "And where do you suppose I would have an opportunity to do something like that?"

Bridget shrugged. "Faye lives on a ranch. What if you ask for her help in exchange for some cheap labor?"

Her suggestion wasn't half-bad. For once, Bridget's nosiness was going to pay off. This could be a win-win situation for both himself and Faye. He just needed to get her to see it.

Before he could tell Bridget thanks for her idea, the mechanic had disappeared into the shop. Adam's father would be back from running his errands pretty soon and maybe Adam could convince him to allow such a trade.

Knowing his father, Sam would be all over this. He always liked doing little acts of service. Not to mention, if it got Adam dating someone again, his dad would likely push him to take part in any activity that entailed.

ADAM PULLED onto the Callahan property, ducking his head to get a better view of the large ranch house. While it was only two stories tall, it still felt like it towered overhead. He'd known the family was well off, which was why this swap still seemed silly. If Faye didn't want to help him, then she could just go begging her father to pay for it.

There was no way that Zeke would tell his own daughter no when it came to something she loved that reminded her of her mother. He was her father. That's what parents were supposed to do.

Then again, Adam had heard plenty of stories regarding the gruff man. Maybe he wasn't that kind of father. It was entirely possible he raised his daughters to be hard workers. Adam couldn't help but feel a small amount of respect for the man.

He put his truck into park and surveyed the area. There were cowboys wandering the premises, leading horses to and from the barn. He didn't see many women working, but that didn't mean they weren't. The one in particular he wanted to speak with should be there based on the presence of the truck he'd looked at earlier in the day.

He shook out his hand, snapping his fingers together to relieve some pressure. There wasn't any reason for him to be nervous. He wasn't here to ask for a handout. The fact that he was asking Faye for help only meant he didn't have to make a fool of himself in front of the multitude of cowboys in this town. The last thing he wanted was to have it get back to Dahlia that he was learning how to ride to impress her. That was one surefire way to have her lose any interest in him whatsoever.

Adam emerged from the truck and headed for the front door. This was a simple offering. Nothing more. He wasn't pitying her, and he definitely wasn't offering anything for free.

So why couldn't he shake this feeling that he should have stepped back and thought this through before coming here?

The door swung open before he had a chance to climb the stairs. Adam froze, his hand on the smooth wood railing as he stared up at the one person he'd come here to see. Faye seemed to be in just as much shock as he was. Her hand remained on the doorknob as if doing so would offer her some semblance of quick escape.

He couldn't blame her. They'd only interacted just the one time, and she'd left in such a hurry that he didn't think they'd be seeing each other again any time soon.

The door behind her clicked closed and she took a step away from it. "Mr. Cullen? What are you doing here? Is there something else wrong with the truck? Because I already told you, I can't—"

"Oh! No, there's nothing else. I did a thorough workup on it." He let out a nervous chuckle and shifted his weight from one foot to the other. "But, to be fair, the workup was pretty bad as it was. Your truck isn't going to be running much longer without those fixes. And the more you drive it, the worse everything is going to become."

Her brows lowered and her lips thinned into a straight line. "So you came here to tell me that my truck is a lost cause unless I ask you to fix it?"

Adam shook his head again. This all sounded so ridiculous in his head. Why couldn't he just get the words out? It hadn't been hard at all to discuss his idea with his father. He would have expected that Bridget would be all over something like this—especially since it was her idea in the first place. But he only got a noncommittal grunt when he announced he was going to take her advice.

"Hello?" Faye's voice broke through his thoughts and he focused on her once more.

"What?"

"Did you come here to rub it in or something? I already told you I can't afford to pay the labor costs."

"Right. Well, I came up with an idea—actually, it was Bridget's idea—but I thought we could work out an arrangement."

She didn't say anything, but the look of pure suspicion on her face was enough to tell him she wasn't one to trust easily. From what he'd heard, she came by it honestly. Zeke was the exact same way.

"Anyway, do you think we could discuss a few options?"

Faye crossed her arms over her chest, still eyeing him. "No one has stopped you so far."

He forced a chuckle. He'd never been intimidated by anyone who had brought in a car to get worked on. And Faye had seemed sweet yesterday. But this sensation he had building in his chest was enough to have him throw his hands in the air and tell her to forget it.

The only movement from Faye was the slow lift of her left eyebrow.

"How about a trade," he blurted.

"A trade."

Adam nodded. "You need your truck worked on. And I would still expect you to help out since I can't have Bridget take time out of her schedule to do it. We could work on it in the evenings or on the weekends, whenever fits your schedule."

"And?" Faye's arms dropped to her sides and she moved to the edge of the porch. They stood only a few feet apart now.

"And... I want to learn how to handle a horse."

Both brows lifted this time. "You don't know how to ride a horse?"

He fought the heat that crept up his neck. He shouldn't feel embarrassed about this. "A lot of people don't know how to ride."

Faye snorted. "Not in Copper Creek."

Adam sighed. "Fine, not in Copper Creek. But it's more than learning to ride. I want to get good enough to enter a competition or the rodeo."

She took one step down closer to him and her lips quirked up at the corners. "Why do you want to learn how to compete? You have a good-paying job. You don't need to be like those rodeo nerds. You realize it's dangerous, don't you?" Her voice was tight, as if his answer would dictate how she felt about him.

He felt the frustration growing. He'd come here to make her an offer and all he got was pushback. "Do you want your truck fixed or not?"

Faye's whole body stiffened and the amusement left her face. "Of course I do."

"Then do you accept my terms?"

She came another step closer. "So let me get this straight. You will fix my car—"

"With your help."

"Right, with my help. If I teach you how to stay on a horse?"

"And help me find an event I can do reasonably well in."

Faye snorted, which wasn't what he'd expected. "When do you want to be able to compete by? I hope you're not dimwitted enough to think that you can just learn how to compete with the big leaguers in a couple weeks. Those people have been riding since they were in diapers. They know their stuff."

"It can't be that hard to hold onto a bucking horse."

She shook her head. "*That's* what you want to compete in? Bronc riding? Are you crazy? No. Forget it. I'm not going to sit back and watch you make a fool of yourself and possibly get killed in the process." She turned to march back up the stairs, but his hand shot out to grasp hers. Faye turned to look at him once more.

"Then teach me to ride and a few techniques."

"What does your dad have to say about this? Or your girlfriend?"

His face heated. "My dad has long since stopped caring what I do. He didn't care when I left town, and he's not going to care if I enter a competition. And I don't have a girlfriend... yet."

Something flickered in her eyes. He wasn't sure what it was, but there was some kind of understanding that passed between them.

"You're doing this to impress a girl, aren't you?"

"So what if I am?" This was the biggest reason he preferred not to spend time with women. They always had to get in his business when it came to dating or other girls. Guys were more straightforward. They'd ask a question here or there, but they never judged him for the answers he gave.

Her eyes dipped to where he still held her hand which prompted him to release her. Faye turned to face him all the way but leaned her hip against the stair railing. "If you need to get bucked off a horse to impress a girl, then she's not the right girl for you."

As hard as he fought it, Adam couldn't help rolling his eyes. "What is it with women and all the judgment? Don't forget that men competing for a woman's attention goes back centuries. Today it might not be duels or jousting, but it's still prevalent. She hangs around tough guys all day—guys who know how to handle horses. So what if I want to throw my hat into the ring? Look, if you're not willing to help me, then your truck doesn't get fixed and I just find someone else who's willing to give me lessons."

Faye studied him as if her next words were going to be the most important ones she'd need to utter. For a moment he thought she would decline just like she had a few minutes ago. But then she let out a resigned sigh. "Fine. I'll teach you about horse riding. But I'm not going to support you getting your butt kicked in the rodeo ring."

"Fine. You don't have to help me learn how to ride a bronco. Just help me figure my way around a saddle and stuff."

She pressed her lips together once more. "You're not going to give up on this, are you? You're still going to try to compete in a rodeo this summer."

He shrugged. "I don't know why that matters."

"Because—" She cut herself off and shook her head. "Never mind. You're right. It doesn't matter. I'll teach you what I can. You do whatever you want."

3

Faye

It had been one week since Faye had agreed to teach Adam to ride a horse, and today was the day he said he'd come by the ranch to get started. Her father was aware of their arrangement, and she couldn't tell if he was upset about any of it. When she'd told him, he'd just grunted and turned back to the magazine he was flipping through.

The agreement Faye had made with Adam suited her just fine. She itched to get out of the house more and more as of late due to how quiet it had become. Adeline still hung around even though she was married and lived in the head-ranch-hand's cabin. But she didn't share meals with them anymore. Half of her sisters were married now, leaving only Brielle, Eloise, Grace and herself—though Grace would be getting married this summer and soon clear out of their childhood home.

These thoughts led her to observe her father a little more.

What would he do when they were all gone? It wasn't too hard to imagine the strict rules he used to force on them were to keep them around just a little longer.

Well, she wasn't going to leave any time soon, so he wouldn't have to worry about being entirely alone for a good couple of years.

Faye kissed the top of his head after clearing her breakfast plate. He offered her a smile and she headed for the door. She didn't have any idea as to how well Adam would take to riding. For all she knew, he'd be just like the newbies down at the Equestrian Therapy Center that Shane ran. Or he could be a natural.

Either way, she didn't think the trade was all that fair. She was getting a great deal more out of it than he was. She just hoped he didn't realize it before he was done fixing her truck.

Right as Faye exited the house, Adam's truck pulled up in the driveway. She slowed and then came to a stop as he climbed out of the truck and headed toward her. Her gaze swept over him from head to toe. He wore a baseball cap, T-shirt, jeans, and tennis shoes. And that's when her cursory check stopped.

Faye gestured at his feet. "You're not wearing those."

He lifted one sneaker then the next. "What? These are my running shoes."

She lifted a brow.

"What's wrong with wearing these?"

"Several things are wrong with wearing tennis shoes." She sighed, placing her hand on her hip. "Do you know how much a horse weighs?"

"I don't know, like five hundred pounds?"

"Try twice that. What do you think will happen to your little toes if the horse you're working with steps on your feet?"

He frowned. Good, he wasn't fighting her.

"On top of the possibility of getting stepped on, we ride with boots to protect our ankles and legs from getting pinched from the saddle. They also have safety heels to help when riding. You can't just wear any boot, and you definitely can't wear those."

"Well, these are all I have. We're going to have to use them until I can get myself a pair of real cowboy boots."

Faye sighed. "Come with me. I'm sure we can find a ranch hand who has a spare pair. I'm not taking you out riding unless you have the right gear. The last thing I need is a lawsuit."

He chuckled, but his grin fled his face when he noticed the sharp look she shot him. "I'm not going to sue you. That's the last thing on my mind."

"Better safe than sorry."

Once Adam had the proper footwear, they headed back to the barn. She strode toward a wall that held various hats and helmets on it. "Now that you have the right shoes, we'll move on to the next most important thing for staying safe. The first thing you should know about horse riding with me is that helmets are non-negotiable." She pulled one from the wall and tossed it at him.

The helmet hit him in the chest and he let out an "oof." Adam turned the helmet in his hands and then gave her a look of disbelief. "You can't be serious."

"Oh, I'm deadly serious."

Adam gestured toward the wall. "What about the cowboy hats? Can't I use one of those?"

She crossed her arms, fighting the urge to smile at him. "Nope. You're a beginner, and as such, you get the helmet." Faye turned toward the aisle that ran down the center of two rows of stalls. "Okay, so you have the right shoes, the right headwear, and now we get to talk about the first rule. Stay alert."

She stopped suddenly and turned to face him, only to have him collide with her. Faye stumbled back a step and her arms went flailing. Adam's hand shot out and grabbed one of them, preventing her from making contact with the concrete flooring.

For the first time since she'd met him, Adam grinned at her like some kind of child. Only the smile he wore wasn't as annoying as she thought it would be. It made her pulse flutter, and the warmth of his hand on her arm caused her nerves to do a little dance. She pushed him away, flustered with the way he was affecting her.

"I told you to stay alert," she accused.

"To be fair, you didn't say 'stay alert because I'm going to stop in the middle of the walking path.' If you had said that, maybe I would have been able to stop before we collided."

Faye frowned at him. "Stay alert means stay alert. You'll be handling a huge animal. One wrong move and you, the horse, or someone else will get hurt. Safety comes first no matter what. I won't be responsible for someone acting like a numbskull."

The grin melted from his face and his jaw clenched before he muttered, "Noted."

"Good. Now, we're going to saddle and harness the horse you'll be riding today. We won't go out on a trail or anything, but you can take a few rounds in the corral."

He gave her a short nod.

Over the next several minutes, she hovered as she gave him orders. She pointed out how to put the saddle on and where to position it on the back of the horse. She made sure he buckled every strap so they were secure but not too tight.

Once he was done, she did the exact same thing with her own horse, asking him what steps she would need to take next.

When they were both ready, she led her horse out of his stall and gestured for Adam to follow her. All that work had gone relatively quick considering he'd never done any of it before. Adam was a quick learner and he listened well. She couldn't help but feel impressed. Most guys she'd interacted with seemed to have a hard time giving women the lead.

They made it to the corral and she tied her horse to the outside before she opened the gate and motioned for him to enter. Adam moved past her and waited in the center of the corral for further instruction—another choice she hadn't expected him to make.

Faye closed the gate, secured it, then strode toward him. "As this is your first time, I'm going to hold the reins while you get into the saddle. We don't want your horse to take off when you've got one foot in the stirrups. Don't think you'd like being dragged along the ground much."

She wasn't sure, but she could have sworn Adam bit back another grin. Was he mocking her? Did he find this humorous? Irritation flooded her stomach, but she pressed forward. Faye strode toward him and he jumped out of the way. She motioned toward the strap beneath the saddle before she grabbed the saddle horn to tug on it. "You always need to check the girth. If it's not secure enough, then the saddle could roll when you're getting on." The saddle didn't move. "And actually, you did a pretty good job."

Adam beamed at her. "I knew I'd be a natural."

She snorted but didn't comment. Just because someone could saddle a horse didn't mean they could ride one. Faye walked around to the left side of the horse and stared at Adam from where she stood. "This is the side you'll mount from. Most horses are accustomed to riders working from the left side. When they can predict what you're going to do, they won't be so skittish."

"Got it."

"You'll put your left foot into the stirrup, lift yourself up into the saddle and sit gently. Then put your right foot into the stirrup and make sure you center the ball of your foot on it."

He nodded, walking around the front of the horse. He held out his reins to her and she took them as she watched to see if he'd follow every one of her instructions.

Adam did everything perfectly. There wasn't a single thing she had to correct—but telling him that would only give him a big head. Once again, that smile touched his lips.

"That wasn't so bad," he said.

"You have a temperate horse. Don't get too cocky."

The horse shifted beneath him and then took a step forward. His free hand darted to the saddle horn, and he gripped it so tight his fingertips turned white. So he wasn't as confident as he made himself out to be.

Faye chuckled and brought the reins up to him. "Okay, now you're going to make her go. Put a small amount of pressure on her with your lower legs. Sometimes she doesn't like to get going with that, so you can do a little bump with your heels. But be soft. She's been trained to go slow, but you still don't want to make her mad."

Adam's horse moved forward, clopping and bobbing her head as she headed past Faye. Adam sat tall in the saddle, and when he came around the bend, he grinned at her like he'd just gotten what he'd always wanted for Christmas.

Faye fell into step beside the horse. "How are you feeling?"

"Great. This is a lot easier than I thought."

She shook her head. "I'm sorry to break it to you, but this is supposed to be easy. There are no competitions where you get to walk around a corral with a retired horse."

"Retired?"

"Of course she's retired. She's pretty old. Do you think I'd put you on a horse that would bolt? Not on your life."

Adam scowled at her with indignation. "I assure you, I can handle myself. This helmet is ridiculous, and this horse is too. When are you going to give me the real lessons I'm supposed to get in our trade?"

She really shouldn't have reacted. That was the stubborn part of her floating to the surface. But she had to drive her point home. Faye stepped in front of his horse, causing her to stop her slow merry-go-round. "Fine. You take my horse and see if you can handle him."

"Really?"

"Really."

Adam didn't even hesitate. He climbed down from the saddle and hurried toward the gate. In a few moments he had brought her horse into the corral and had mounted him. Next thing Faye knew, Adam was heading around the corral. There was a split second between the time he gave her that look and the moment he really dug his heels into the sides of her horse that she realized what he intended to do. But by the time that happened, it was too late. Her horse took off, causing Adam to nearly fall off the back of the saddle. He corrected his stance while holding onto the saddle horn.

The way his rump collided with the saddle each time her horse hit a specific rhythm made it clear she'd have to teach him how to move with the horse rather than against it. She almost felt bad for what she was going to do next as her eyes followed him around the corral with each lap he took.

"Okay," she called. "Pull him to a stop."

Adam glanced in her direction then pulled on the reins. What she expected to happen did. He'd pulled too hard. The horse reacted, the bit in his mouth being tugged too far back.

He reared up on his hind legs and shook his head. The movement surprised Adam enough that he managed to let go of the reins, saddle horn, and any contact he had with the saddle.

He tumbled backward and landed in the dirt with a hard thud.

Faye hurried toward the horse, but she already knew he wouldn't do anything now that his rider had been displaced. He wandered lazily toward the horse Adam had ridden first.

Adam was on his back, his eyes staring up into the blue sky overhead. His chest rose and fell, and he coughed a few times. When she leaned over his body, his eyes found hers. "What was that?" he wheezed.

"What was what?"

"Why did he do that?"

She placed both hands on her hips. "Well, would you like it if someone yanked on a piece of metal in your mouth?"

Adam groaned as he sat up. "I suppose not."

"That's exactly what you did. You have to remember to treat these horses with respect. What you did could have made him skittish around not only you but other people, too. You're lucky he didn't continue bucking when he got you off." A smile touched her lips. "But you know there's one good thing about what just happened?"

"And what's that?"

"Now you know what you're up against if you decide to compete in the rodeo. Only next time you won't have a helmet." She still couldn't believe he was sticking to his guns on this. It didn't matter how many times she told him it wasn't a good idea; this guy just wasn't getting it.

Adam rolled his eyes and held his hand out to her.

She helped to pull him to his feet. "Okay, now get back in the saddle."

"What? Don't you want me to get on *my* horse?"

Faye shook her head. "When it comes to riding, my father always insisted on one thing. When you fall out of the saddle, you get back on the horse."

"Everyone says that," he muttered. "Only no one knows what it's like to do it literally."

4

Adam

Adam still couldn't seem to catch his breath. The impact he'd made on the hard dirt had managed to lodge his lungs into places they didn't belong. The worst part was that Faye had been completely right and now he had egg on his face, not to mention a bruised tailbone. His head pounded, pulsating with each beat his heart took.

He scowled at her from his perch on the saddle. "I thought that the helmet was supposed to prevent me from getting hurt."

She smirked at him, and as much as he thought he'd hate that knowing smile, he couldn't help but think she looked absolutely adorable. Faye moved closer to him and ran her hand down the horse's shoulder. "Well, your head didn't break open, did it? You didn't die, did you?" Then before he had a chance to realize what she was doing, she slapped her hand on her horse's rump.

The horse took off like it had before, and this time his heart raced but not from exhilaration. It pounded like nothing he'd ever felt before. His breath caught in his lungs and it took every ounce of control not to shut his eyes against what was happening.

The rhythm of the horse's hooves thundered against the ground but with a more even tempo. The longer he let the horse go, the less terrified he became. This was okay. He could do this. The only problem at this point was figuring out how to stop without pulling too hard on the reins. Oh... *and* trying to prevent the damage that the saddle hitting his backside would cause.

He caught sight of Faye standing in the center of the corral with the horse he now wished he'd stuck with. The smile she sported was a combination of excitement and wicked intent. The way she looked in that moment, he could see her being cast as an evil queen in some child's fairytale.

Faye cupped her hand next to her mouth. Her voice sounded distant even though they were close enough that she could have spoken at a regular level. "Now, when you want to slow down, you have to be gentle. You can't just yank on the reins. Don't pull them too close or too tight. You need to give him some breathing room."

"Easy for you to say," he called back. "My lungs still haven't gotten back to normal capacity."

She laughed, and it was the most beautiful sound he'd ever heard. Adam nearly lost his focus when he glanced toward her to see if she, indeed, was the source of that laughter. Faye gestured with her hands as if he could see what she was doing.

"You need to tug gently, then release and tell him 'whoa.' He knows what that means."

Adam gripped the saddle with one hand and the reins with the other. He tugged on the rope a little. "Whoa."

The horse slowed rather than coming to a complete halt. He tossed his head and shifted around in a circle, probably still antsy from the last time he'd tried something similar.

Adam's head snapped up and he grinned at Faye. "I did it."

She wandered toward him, her smile matching his. "You're a quick learner—though you need to trust me a little more." One brow lifted and she gave him a pointed look. "You should trust your horse, too. The ones you'll be riding here have had extensive training. They only need the barest touch to know what they're expected to do. We can't have horses that have minds of their own."

Faye's soft smile returned to her face and she traced her hand down the horse's neck again. "Blaze here has been with the family since he was a baby. He can do everything from rounding up animals to barrel racing and dressage competitions." Her gaze flitted to his. "But that doesn't mean he doesn't have an attitude every so often. He doesn't like it when people are rough with him. Treat him with respect, and he'll do the same to you."

"Blaze, huh?"

She nodded. "I picked him out when I was younger. I got to help with his training. He's super smart, but times like today he can be a real pain in the..." Her cheeks colored. "Well, you know."

Adam rubbed his backside. "Yeah. I think I get what you're saying."

Her focus shifted to the barn for a moment then she brought it back to him. "I know I said we weren't going to go out for a ride, but if you're up for it, you can get back on your horse and we can see how you do on a trail."

"On my horse? That one?" He nodded toward the horse

that still stood in the center of the corral. "What's her name anyway?"

"She's Bella. And we'd strictly be walking on this one."

Putting all the weight on one stirrup, Adam climbed down from the saddle. His legs didn't seem to want to come together. The way he walked, it felt like he was still seated on that hard surface.

Faye giggled. "Yeah, that's gonna happen a lot. It's what they mean when they say you're walking bow-legged. Welcome to cowboy life. This is what you wanted, right?"

Adam gave her a dark look as he passed. "This? No. I didn't want any of what happened today."

"Nothing? What about those exciting moments? Like when you got the saddle on and when you got Blaze to stop?"

"Okay, that was fine. But I didn't sign on for this helmet or the way my whole body is aching." Just saying it out loud seemed to make his body hurt more. Every muscle, every joint, every bone, heck... every hair on his head seemed to cry out in agony. He thought he was in good shape. But apparently working on cars didn't help much with that sort of thing.

The effort it took to lift one booted foot into the stirrup was far harder than he expected. He let out a groan and then shook his head and put his foot down. "Nope. I can't do it. I'm gonna have to tap out for today."

Adam glanced at Faye, expecting to see disappointment of some kind but couldn't get a read on her. He stretched out his legs for lack of anything else he could do. And then attempted to stretch his back. Pain radiated everywhere from the top of his head right down to his toenails. If this was what riding was like, he wasn't so sure he'd be able to handle it, and he'd been injured in more ways than he could count while working on cars.

Faye nodded. "Sure, if that's what you want."

They wandered in silence side by side toward the barn, each leading their own horse. Only Adam was limping and he didn't even know why. It wasn't like his feet were the biggest problem.

Everything was made ten times worse when he realized he had to remove Bella's saddle and brush her down. Either he needed to get in better shape, or he needed to find a different way to connect with Dahlia.

"For what it's worth, you did a pretty good job out there." Her voice was quiet, more encouraging than she'd been since their lesson had started.

Adam glanced in her direction, not sure what to make of it. She could just be trying to make him feel better. And if that were the case, he didn't want any of it. He let out a grunt as he continued running the brush from one end of his horse to the other.

"It was a first attempt. I didn't expect to be an expert by the end of today," he said.

"Don't let today's experiences get you down."

"I didn't say I was upset about anything."

"Excuse me for sensing you're a little disappointed." The defensive tone returned to her voice. "You're the one who wanted to learn, and it's not my fault if you didn't have the right expectations for what would happen on your first day. But just so you know, I'm not backing down from the deal we made. I want my mom's truck fixed. So if you decide to quit—"

Adam spun to face her fully. "I'm *not* a quitter. Geez. What kind of folk have you been interacting with around here? Do people quit that easily?"

"Well, no... but—"

"The way you're talking, I would have assumed they did. I'm not quitting just because one horse knocked me on my backside. Our next meeting will be at the shop. You need to come prepared to get dirt under your fingernails." His gaze swept over her. "Working on cars isn't easy either. Maybe you need to bring a helmet too."

She stared at him for what felt like an entire minute before the corners of her lips quirked into a grin. "You're joking."

"Yeah. I am. Don't be so serious all the time. This whole thing we've got going here isn't really that sort of situation. You're helping me, and I'm helping you. We can be friendly, alright? And for goodness sake, don't treat me like some weakling from the city. I may have spent some time there, but I was born and raised in Copper Creek. I can handle myself just fine." A few bumps and bruises weren't enough to make him quit—at least not yet. Adam turned back to the task at hand, but when he shot a look in her direction, he noticed she seemed a bit more at ease.

Faye was something else. She was the kind of girl he would have expected to have been spoiled all her life and wanted everything given to her. The fact that she was willing to roll up her sleeves and do hard work was a breath of fresh air. Though he shouldn't have been surprised. The women who were raised in this part of town were usually like that. They had to be or nothing would get done.

Back in Colorado Springs, women were vastly different. He'd been on his fair share of dates to know that they weren't made the same out there. Granted, not all of the city girls were the same, but a heck of a lot of them had zero interest in doing the kind of work that built character. He'd met several that still lived with their parents or still got allowances from their folks. He always wondered what might happen if their parents passed away suddenly.

How would they survive?

If heaven forbid something drastic happened to Faye's

father, he didn't have a doubt in his mind that she would survive.

He cleared his throat, causing her to meet his gaze. "Mind if I ask you something?"

Faye shrugged. "I guess. But it doesn't mean I'll answer."

Adam chuckled. Comments like those were part of the reason he knew she was different. "Why is this truck so important?"

"I already told you—"

"It was your mother's. I know. But why would you go to so much trouble to keep it? Why not take some pictures of it and stick them in a photo album or something?"

Her brushing slowed as she contemplated his question. Or maybe she was trying to figure out a way to tell him to jump off a cliff in a nice way. Either way, waiting for her to respond managed to make him feel even more uncomfortable. He shouldn't have pried. He didn't know what it was like to lose someone, let alone a parent.

Faye finally placed the brush aside and faced him. "My earliest memory of my mother was in that truck."

It took everything inside him not to react. He wasn't entirely certain of her age when her mother had passed, but he couldn't imagine that she'd been very old. She was the second-to-youngest in this family. She was probably around three or four at the time if his memory served him correctly.

"Every so often she would take us out... my sisters and me. She'd take us one at a time. I don't recall all the times she did it. But my dad would tell me stories. My mom wanted to make sure each of us felt special and loved. I guess every time she put me in the truck, I wanted the same thing."

Adam's eyes started to get misty.

Faye nodded. "It's silly. I get it. Why hold onto something

so old and pay so much when all I have are bare snippets of memories that, for all I know, could be dreams."

"It's not silly." He moved closer to her, closing the gap. The only thing between them was the stall wall that came up to his chest. "There are far more frivolous things, I assure you. That isn't to say that this truck is a *smart* thing to invest in." Adam chuckled. "But it's not silly."

She offered him a grateful smile. "Thanks. You don't know how much I needed to hear that right now."

"Sure. One more thing."

"Yeah?"

"Will my body be in this much pain *all* the time?"

"No." Faye snickered, that beautiful laugh that made his insides tingle and the ache dissipate, even if it was briefly.

Adam grinned. It was strange feeling this way—loving the fact that he could make her laugh. He didn't care about making Bridget laugh—or anyone else besides Dahlia. Some small part of him felt connected to Faye. It was almost like he felt the need to protect her or be there for her in a way he didn't feel he needed to for anyone else.

Maybe that was one of the reasons he accepted Bridget's idea so easily. There were plenty of cowboys who came to the shop to get their equipment fixed, and not once had he considered a trade of services before.

But it wasn't because he *liked* Faye. Not in that way, at least. No. It was something else.

He *liked* Dahlia. That was the whole reason he was doing any of this. The way he felt drawn to Faye was definitely different. It was a kinship of sorts, and it was just nice that he'd found a friend in the process.

$$5$$

Faye

Faye couldn't remember a time when she'd had more fun teaching someone about the basics of riding. There was something about hanging out with Adam that made her feel good inside. She couldn't put her finger on it, but that thought crossed her mind several times over the next week.

She found herself looking forward to seeing him again, which was completely crazy. She wasn't interested in him romantically, and he definitely wasn't interested in her that way either. He was interested in someone else. That's what he came here for, to learn how to ride so he could impress a girl.

They couldn't be considered friends, not when the only time they spent together was her teaching him how not to fall off a horse.

Faye let out a soft laugh under her breath as she sat at the kitchen table, garnering a curious look from her father. His gaze lingered and she shook her head, turning her attention back to her scrambled eggs.

Adam had messaged her yesterday that the parts he'd needed for her truck were in, so she'd be taking it to the shop. The way her heart fluttered ever so slightly at the thought did give her pause, though. There was nothing to be nervous about. Adam seemed like a good enough mechanic. Her truck was in good hands.

When she glanced up at her father again, she found his gaze on her. It was that discerning stare he always used when he was trying to figure something out without asking too many questions.

Faye pushed away from the table, and her sisters glanced in her direction before returning their focus to their meals. "What?"

Zeke's brows lifted and he shook his head. "I didn't say anything."

Brielle didn't even have to tear her focus from the phone in her hand. "You never have to say anything, Dad. We can tell just by the way you look at us that something's on your mind." Her dry voice broke through that awkward silence that hung between Faye and her father.

He shifted in his seat, putting his fork down on the table. "If I don't ask a question, then I don't need an answer."

Brielle snorted. "Either you're in denial or you don't see the way you've trained us to practically give you any and all information you want just by giving us *that* look." She finally lifted her gaze from her phone and winked at Faye before turning a sweet smile to her father. "It's never *nothing* with you, but that's okay. Don't worry. We love you anyway." She stood from the table and kissed the top of his head before she took her plate to the sink. "Besides, we all know why you're looking at Faye that way."

He stiffened, his attention shifting to Brielle rather than Faye. "You can't possibly know what I'm thinking about."

Brielle laughed. "Really? Like you don't react in the exact same way when a new guy enters our lives? It doesn't even have to be a guy we're interested in. Any time fresh testosterone enters the mix, you're all over it." She gave Faye a meaningful look. "Just be careful, okay?"

Faye didn't know how to respond. This conversation had taken on a life of its own. Luckily, she got her wits about her before Brielle left the kitchen. "I don't have to be careful. I'm not doing anything dangerous."

Her older sister shrugged as she strode toward the door. "I guess I assumed wrong."

"Just what did you assume? There's nothing going on with me." Faye followed her sister out of the kitchen, mildly grateful she was no longer being scrutinized by her father. The way he continued to look at her was unnerving, to say the least.

Brielle didn't stop walking. She continued through the house toward her room, not answering the question. Faye had to pick up her pace in order to stay in step with her sister.

"Really, Bri. I'm not doing anything dangerous. I don't know why you had to say that in front of Dad. Now he's gonna think I'm up to something, and we all know that's not my MO; it's yours."

Her sister stopped, turning to face Faye abruptly. "That wasn't a very nice thing to say."

"Well, what you said back there wasn't very nice either. Now I'm going to have to explain to him why you think I'm doing something wrong."

"No, you won't. Didn't you hear me? I retracted what I said." Brielle's features were flat and unexpressive. She was hiding something, but what, Faye had no idea. She wasn't close enough to Brielle to know how to dig up whatever it was she didn't want to share. Brielle let out a sigh. "Sorry I said anything, okay?" She brushed past Faye, leaving her with more questions than answers.

Faye turned to head back to the kitchen when she nearly had a heart attack. Grace stood in the hallway, leaning against the wall as casually as an old-school western cowboy. "Don't worry about her. She just went through a breakup."

"Who said I was worried? Brielle always acts weird. Wait, she was dating someone?"

Grace cocked her head slightly. "Yeah. I guess that is the weird part. She was dating someone and it didn't work out. She said she's fine and that it's for the best, but I think it hurt her a little more this time."

"But I didn't see anyone coming around."

"That's the way she does it. Brielle doesn't like the attention because she knows it's gonna be a big deal. Then if it doesn't work out, she's left with nothing."

Faye shot a look over her shoulder to where Brielle had disappeared to. "Who was she dating?"

This time Grace let out a laugh. "She would kill me if I told you. The only reason I know is because I sorta set them up in the first place."

"I didn't think Brielle was capable of having her heart broken," she murmured.

"Faye!"

She grimaced. "You know that's not what I meant. Brielle is the one who always breaks up with people. Do we even know if she was the one who was broken up with? We all know she's gone through her share of guys. She's never *serious* with anyone. Not really."

Grace pushed away from the wall and strode toward Faye, her gaze hardened. "Just because she's the one breaking up with someone doesn't mean she doesn't feel the loss. How would you feel if you were in her position? She's watched her older sister and younger sisters all get engaged and married, and she's left behind."

Faye snorted. "Are you forgetting that I'm one of the sisters who isn't married yet? I'm seeing everyone start dating, too, and I'm not all torn up over it."

"Yeah, but you're not dating anyone. You don't have anything you're hoping will turn into something more. Bri was just warning you not to get too attached to Adam, that's all."

"Attached to *Adam*?" Faye let out a strangled laugh. Had she toyed with the idea that in a different life they might have been more? Sure. What girl wouldn't when the guy could make her laugh so easily? But she'd already figured out where they stood with each other. "I'm *not* interested in Adam at all. Not only that, but he's only helping me with my truck because he's getting something out of it."

"Yeah, we all saw how you two were getting along last week." Grace's lips curled into a mocking grin. "We're not blind, Faye. We can tell what's really going on."

Faye threw her hands into the air. "Is that what this is all about? You think that just because I'm teaching him how to ride that, suddenly, I won't be able to control myself? You think I'm going to fall in love with him?"

Grace's pointed look was all it took to confirm Faye's question.

"Well, tough luck. It's not gonna happen. Adam has a huge crush on some girl in the rodeo circuit. He wants to impress her with his horsemanship abilities. Too bad it's gonna take a ton of work for him to even come close to the guys he's comparing himself to."

"Really? You actually believe that?"

Faye stared at her sister, dumbfounded. "What is that supposed to mean?"

"Adam could have gotten anyone to teach him how to ride. You do realize that he's the only mechanic in town. And there are several others who are more qualified to teach him how to ride. He could have made this trade with anyone. So why did he pick you?"

Her mouth opened but no words came. She snapped it shut and then attempted again, only for her brain to let her down again. A mixture of a growl and groan burst from her chest, and she stomped toward the kitchen.

"I'd follow Bri's advice if I were you. Be careful," Grace's voice called after her, but Faye refused to acknowledge what she said. She was wrong. They were all wrong and she'd prove it.

Faye came skidding to a stop right before she entered the kitchen. She didn't want to have to feel her father's judgmental stare on her. She turned on her heel and headed for the front door instead. She didn't need her boots. She'd be working on her truck, not riding. All she needed were her tennis shoes and her keys.

THE WHOLE WAY TO TOWN, Faye argued with herself. Grace had made one good point she couldn't find an explanation for. Adam had picked her to help him with his training. Why would he do that? He didn't know her except that she was a Callahan. Just because she knew horses didn't mean she'd be a good rider or even a good teacher.

Yes, she thought she was, but that didn't mean anything.

Adam hadn't shown any interest in her. He hadn't made any moves or comments. And all the messages he'd texted her were related to fixing the truck or setting up the first riding lesson. Grace and Brielle were just trying to mess with her. That's what this had to be.

Faye pulled into the parking lot of the mechanic's shop and put the truck into park. She climbed out and headed straight for the entrance and right up to the counter where Adam stood.

"You don't like me, do you?"

He stared at her like she was crazy.

And maybe she was.

One thing was for certain, she didn't like beating around the bush, which sometimes got her in trouble, and as it turned out, this was one of those times.

He glanced to the person beside her—someone she hadn't even registered was there in the first place. "I'm sorry about that. Here's your invoice. We changed the oil, topped off your wiper fluid and brake fluid, and cleaned out your filter. You've probably got another ten thousand miles before you should consider replacing that. Otherwise, your truck is in good shape."

Faye glanced at the older man as she scooted away from him. Her face was completely flooded with a searing heat, so hot it was almost painful. The guy let out a chuckle as he nodded toward her before he headed for the door.

As soon as the door shut, Adam turned to her. "Okay, now what's this about you thinking I don't like you?" A smile tugged at his lips, and her blush intensified.

Faye swallowed hard and dropped her gaze. This was so embarrassing. Why did she have to realize her mistakes *after* she blurted everything she shouldn't? There had to be a better way for her to bring up this concern. "Okay, first off, sorry about that."

He chuckled again. "No problem."

"Second of all, my sisters have gotten it in their heads that you only offered to help me with the truck because you wanted to spend time with me. I told them that's not true. I told them you have a thing for some rodeo chick."

His eyes danced with amusement. "You're correct. I do have a thing for a rodeo chick."

"Then why did you make me this offer? There are better teachers out there."

Adam moved around the reception counter and leaned his hip against it, his arms crossed over his chest. The way he could just stand there so casually, looking so ruggedly tantalizing... her heart flipped, but then she put a stop to that right away.

No. She wasn't going to look at him that way. He wasn't available, and she wasn't interested in finding love. There was too much drama at home for that to be a good idea.

Adam tilted his head to the side, allowing the tension in the air to build. He was teasing her. He knew he had the upper hand, and he was willing to make her squirm because he liked it.

She folded her arms and nearly stomped her foot—but that would have been childish. Instead, her eyes narrowed. "Will you just give me an answer so I can prove my sisters wrong?"

"I suppose I made the deal with you because it made sense."

"That doesn't answer anything. Think about it. I'm a girl."

"Yeah... So?"

"Spending extra time with me... wouldn't that make her think that you're taken?"

Adam's crooked grin made her insides melt once more. "Honestly? I didn't come up with this plan until Bridget mentioned how much you wanted this truck fixed. You needed something and I needed something. It was a win-win. Anyone else might not care enough to agree to such an arrangement, you know?"

Well, at least that made more sense. She could use his explanation, though chances were slim that Grace and Brielle would just accept it at face value. Her hands dropped to her sides, the fire that had built within her simmering into something else. "Okay."

"Okay? Can we drop this subject now? Because I got the parts to fix your truck. And since you have no idea what we're doing, I'm basically gonna be doing this on my own with your assistance. You know what the names of tools are, right? Or am I going to have to start at the very beginning and teach you what a screwdriver does?"

The lingering warmth in her face pulsed but only slightly. "I was raised by a father who didn't have sons. I think I can handle giving you the tools you ask for."

"Good. Let's get started." He nodded his head toward the front door. "I'm going to open the garage. You pull your truck into the bay."

6

Adam

This girl was undeniably the most interesting girl Adam had ever met. One second she was spitting and hissing like an angry little kitten, and the next she was as sweet as a playful puppy dog. He couldn't tell if his intrigue should be replaced with concern. Had he entered into a deal with a woman who would turn on him?

It was a good thing he wasn't interested in her in a romantic capacity. That would make for a far more difficult arrangement.

Only now that she'd mentioned it, there was a part of him that entertained the idea—not seriously, though. He wasn't dumb enough to get involved with her. That curious part of him would just have to be okay with their friendship.

Faye climbed out of the truck and tossed him the keys. "I guess you get to take these for a while, huh?"

Adam caught the bundle with one hand. "We won't be

using them any time soon. It takes a normal crew with all the right tools around twelve hours on average to replace the engine. Longer since you don't have any experience and I have to teach you a few things."

"What about the transmission?" She glanced at the truck behind her, letting her hand trail over the edge of the hood. "You said we had to do that too?"

He nodded. "That's even longer. It's more complicated, and it can take anywhere from three to five days. But seeing as we're working on the truck just on weekends, it's gonna take a couple months before we get it done."

"A few months?" Her head snapped around to look at him. "I'm going to be without a truck for a few months?"

"I guess you'll have to go back to what you did before your sister gave it to you. That's what happened, right? Grace owned this truck first?"

Faye's disappointed sigh tugged at him more than he'd like to admit. If he could have offered her a rental while they worked on it, he would have. That just wasn't something he had available. She didn't respond to his question, so he let it drop. Faye was an adult. She'd figure something out.

His focus shifted to her clothes. The T-shirt and jeans she wore looked far too nice for her to be working with oil and the like. Adam let out a chuckle, drawing her attention.

"What?"

"It's your turn to put on something you're going to hate."

Her brows creased and her eyes narrowed. "You were joking about that helmet."

"Yes. But the clothes you're wearing aren't going to be the best when you're working with motor oil."

She looked down at her clothes. "These are old. I'm fine with them getting dirty."

"Did you bring a change of clothes?"

"No, why would I do that?"

He shook his head. "I guess there are a few things we both had to learn." He headed for a large cabinet and pulled out a pair of coveralls that were already stained. In one swift motion, he tossed them at her. "Put these on over your clothes. That way when you're done, you can take them off and you don't have to track anything into the vehicle you're taking home."

Faye held the coveralls and a look of distaste crossed her face, but it was immediately replaced with wide eyes. "Shoot. I forgot to ask if my sister could pick me up. Oh great. Neither one of them is gonna want to do that today."

"Why wouldn't your sisters want to help you?" He asked the question out of habit, not really expecting her to answer.

"I got in a fight with them this morning."

He glanced at her. "You want to talk about it?"

She gave him a pointed look. "We sorta did already, remember?"

Understanding washed over him. "The part about whether or not I like you."

"Bingo. Yeah, only two of my sisters who currently live at home have vehicles. And they're the two I decided to pick a fight with. So I'm stuck." She groaned. "I don't want to call an Uber."

"I can take you." The offer slipped from his lips before he was able to consider the consequences of such an offer. Faye shot a surprised look in his direction. Great. That wasn't something he should have said. She'd probably just tell him no anyway. She wouldn't want her sisters to tease her about their weird relationship.

"Are you sure?"

Okay, he was wrong. "Yeah. Why not?"

"I promise I'll make sure I get a ride next time," Faye

murmured as she climbed into her coveralls and pulled the zipper up to her neck. Even though that was the suit Bridget had worn in the past, it completely drowned Faye from head to toe. She'd pulled the sleeves to her wrist, but they didn't have elastic and would need to be rolled up just like her pants.

She got a good look at herself and let out a laugh which only spurred his own laughter. "At least you don't have to wear some silly helmet."

Faye pointed an accusing finger at him. "It wasn't silly. That thing probably saved your life because of your rash choices."

"Point taken." He returned to the cabinet and pulled out a matching blue cap. Ignoring her protests, he slapped the hat onto her head and stood back. She was adorable. How she could make that suit look good was beyond him.

It was time to stop allowing his thoughts to stray from where they ought to be. Adam moved toward the driver's side door. Apparently, Faye didn't realize he needed to access the hood release. She ended up backing up as if doing so, she'd be out of his way. Pressed up against her truck, she looked up at him with wide eyes. Her eyes were green like the pine trees that grew in the Colorado forests. The deep coloring made her eyes seem even bigger than they already were, and for a moment he was mesmerized by them. Then she blinked and broke the trance.

He gestured toward the door she blocked. "I need to get in there."

She released a breath and scooted to the side. "Right. Of course."

Adam peeked at her as she tucked a strand of hair behind her ear and put even more distance between them. "The first thing we have to do is remove the hood. It's gonna take both of us. You think you can handle that?"

Faye nodded. "Sure."

He pulled the release and the hood popped open. It was easy to find the latch, and he was able to lift the hood without much hassle.

"So is there a button I have to push?"

Adam gave her a crooked grin. "If only it was so easy. No. We have to disconnect the clips holding the wiring to the hood. Then we remove the hoses for the wipers. After that. There are a couple fasteners holding the hood to the truck and we have to take those out. Then we'll take the hood off."

Her eyes bounced to the truck and then to him. "That's a lot."

"And that's just the beginning of this whole process." His cocky attitude got the better of him and he adjusted his voice to make it sound like the guy from that karate movie. "Stick with me, grasshopper, and I will make you a master in the art of mechanics."

Faye's next laugh came out in more of a snort, causing her to cover her mouth with her hand. She glanced at him, her whole body ducking, and she laughed again. "I'm sorry. It wasn't supposed to come out like that."

"I like your laugh."

She sobered, straightening as she stared at him with an unreadable expression.

He let out a cough and headed around the front of the truck to start disconnecting wires. "Let's get the hood off and then we can start on the next thing."

While he worked, Faye hovered. She handed him the tools he asked for, all while chatting about some of her sisters. He'd only known of Constance when he was in school, but that was because they shared a math class together and she was one of the smartest people in the room. As he kept to himself most of the time, he didn't really get to know many of the rancher's kids. He spent more time with his dad working on cars than playing with kids his age.

At the rate Faye talked, he had a hard time keeping up with which sister married whom or things about their personalities. It put into perspective just how small his family was. He only had two brothers, both of whom had moved away around the same time he had. Neither of them had gone into mechanics, which was why he was the only one to come back.

He gestured toward the right side of the hood. "Okay. You're going to hold that steady while I take care of this last bolt. Then we're going to take it off."

Faye followed directions immediately, though it did unnerve him slightly that her gaze remained trained on him while he worked. Normally he'd do his work alone or with very little help. Perhaps that was the reason for his discomfort.

With the final bolt removed, he grasped the hood and they lifted it from the truck. Together they walked to the side of the garage and placed it carefully on the floor.

Faye smiled brightly at him, dusting her hands on the coveralls. "Okay! What's next."

"Now, we wait."

"What do you mean?" She looked over to the truck. "Aren't we supposed to start disconnecting things for the engine? Or jack up the truck or something?"

He chuckled. "Patience. If we start digging in right now, we're only going to end up burned. We have to let the engine cool. Then we have to drain the fluids."

"Oh."

They stood there in silence until he couldn't handle it anymore. Did she run out of things to talk about? "How about we go get a coffee down the street?" Before she could decline, he continued. "My treat. It'll only be a little while. Then we can get back to work."

"Okay. Just let me—" She reached for the zipper of her coveralls, and he shook his head. "Don't worry about that. The coffee place I go to, no one's gonna care about what you're wearing." He headed for the door, but when he didn't hear her behind him, he stopped to look back at her.

"I'm not going out in public in this."

He gave her a funny look. "Come on. Live life on the wild side. No one is gonna recognize you anyway. Who are you trying to impress?"

"No one. But—"

"Then come on. We don't have all day. We need to get back and start draining that oil." This time he charged through the door without checking to see if she followed. Either she'd come with him, or she wouldn't, and there was a good chance that she would want to stay here alone even less than she would want to head out in her coveralls.

He was right.

Together they walked briskly down the street. He had his hands shoved into his pockets, glancing at her out of the corner of his eye as they went. Anyone passing would probably just assume she was Bridget. The folks in town all knew and liked his coworker, probably more than they liked him. The men definitely preferred working with Bridget more than they liked working with any Cullen.

"Tell me more about this girl."

He shot a surprised look in her direction. "Who?"

"The girl you're trying to impress. You haven't said anything about her except that you think she wants a guy who's willing to risk his life on the back of an angry horse."

The sigh that burst from his chest did nothing to relieve the pressure he felt building there. He rubbed the back of his neck and glanced at her sideways. He should have known better than to assume that Faye would leave him be on this topic. All women in this town gossiped. Even his mother joined in occasionally. It was what they did.

"Come on. Maybe I can help."

Now that was an idea. Faye was a girl. She worked on a ranch. And tough guys were always around her. She might have some insights that he hadn't considered. Then again, did he really want her knowing who he had a crush on? Not particularly. Given her habit of oversharing, that might not be such a good idea.

"I'm not going to tell you who she is."

"I didn't ask you to."

"Yes, you did."

She groaned. "I did *not*. I asked you to tell me more about her. What does she like? What are her hobbies? I assume you've figured this sort of thing out already. Have you asked her on a date yet?"

"Geez. What's with the third degree?"

There was something else about Faye that took him off guard. She didn't just have one smile. She had several. This one wasn't quite like the one she wore when she was embarrassed, though it was similar. She looked away and gnawed on her lower lip. "Sorry. My sisters tell me I can be a bit much sometimes." When she peeked at him again, that familiar ripple of *something* coursed down his spine. "You don't have to tell me if you don't want to. But I figured since you're helping me out so much, I should probably be doing a little more."

"What you're doing is just fine." They had arrived at the coffee shop, and he pulled the door open for her to enter first. When she brushed past him, he was inundated by the scent of her perfume or shampoo—whatever it was that made her smell like a field of wildflowers.

Adam nearly asked her what it was, but he turned at that

very moment and nearly bumped into none other than Dahlia Johansson.

She looked up into his eyes briefly before smiling and murmuring an apology. "I'm sorry."

Momentarily losing his train of thought, he mumbled something that sounded like gibberish which only made Dahlia scrunch up her face in confusion. He turned to watch her slip out the door and down the street, leaving him feeling like the idiot he was.

"*Wow*," Faye drawled. "Was that her?" Her voice came directly behind him, and he cringed before turning to face her.

"If you must know, yeah. That was her."

Faye tipped so she could look around him. "She's cute." With that final remark, she spun around and strode toward the counter.

7

Faye

Faye hated the way the disappointment flooded her chest. The girl Adam liked was beautiful. She had perfect skin, lush black hair, and deep blue eyes. From what Faye could tell, she was toned, just like any rodeo competitor would be.

No wonder Adam didn't have any interest in Faye. She wasn't as tall as that woman. Her hair was thinner and blonde. And she was a twig. If Adam had a type, it wasn't anything close to Faye.

Whatever. Hadn't she told her sisters over and over that Adam wasn't interested? This just confirmed it. The way he froze up in front of that girl showed just how he acted when he was starstruck.

Faye heaved a sigh just as Adam came to stand beside her. He didn't say anything, and the tension between them continued to thicken. As to why she felt so awkward suddenly, it was hard to say.

Was it possible that she wanted him to like her a little more than he did? Had she developed some sort of attraction for him?

It was entirely possible.

Shoot!

That wasn't supposed to happen.

Okay, this was fine. It was totally fine. It was just a silly crush. That's all. People had crushes all the time that didn't amount to anything. She snuck a glance at him. What was it about Adam that had caught her attention in the first place? When had this attraction even started?

None of that mattered anymore. What was done was done. She'd just have to focus on helping Adam get the girl then maybe she'd get past it.

Yep. That would work.

He turned to look at her and she froze. Had he caught her staring at him? What was she thinking? Of course he did. She could tell, especially due to the small smile that tugged at his lips. Faye clasped her hands together in front of her and glanced at him out of the corner of her eye. "I'm curious about something."

"What's that?"

"Why haven't you spoken to her?"

If the air could have gotten colder with one look, it did at that moment. She'd thought the tension had been heavy before, but now she knew better. "Why do you think I haven't spoken to her?"

She lifted a shoulder. "Well, by the way you couldn't get out a word at all... that spoke for itself. I was under the impression she at least knew who you were."

"Dahlia knows who I am. I've talked to her a few times.

She came in with her brother when he brought in his truck a few weeks ago."

Faye bit back a laugh. This wasn't funny, not really. She shouldn't find any of this humorous at all. And yet there was a part of her that did, in fact, find this amusing. "So she knows who you are, but have you said anything to her that wasn't related to fixing cars?"

"Of course I have. That's how I found out she likes to do barrel racing."

Faye turned to face him, her brows lifting. "You like a barrel racing girl?"

"Yeah, so?"

She pinched the bridge of her nose. "Please tell me you got to know her a little more than that."

His face scrunched into a small frown. "What's your problem with barrel racers?"

"It's not that she's a barrel racer, not really. Though most of the barrel racers I know aren't the nicest people."

He opened his mouth, but before he could argue the barista at the counter called them up. "Next."

Faye hesitated. She should let him say his piece. But there was a growing line behind them, and she really didn't want to have to tell him the stuff she'd heard and seen from the women in that career. There was a chance Dahlia wasn't a career competitor. But based on what she'd heard, that wasn't likely.

"Next!" she repeated.

Faye lurched forward. "I'll take an iced caramel latte."

Adam loomed beside her, and for the first time she felt very small. She'd managed to turn this nice morning into something incredibly uncomfortable. She was a terrible person. Why couldn't she just learn how to keep her mouth shut or at least read the room? She was so wrapped up in her self-loathing that she didn't even hear Adam place his order.

He nudged her, ripping her from her thoughts and nodded toward the side of the shop. "We need to let everyone else order."

She stiffened. "Wait, you paid for mine? You didn't have to do that."

Despite the way he must have been feeling, the corners of his mouth twitched upward. "I told you before. It was my treat."

"Oh yeah," she murmured.

"And just so you know, Dahlia is plenty nice. I might not have had more than two conversations with her—"

"I'm sure you're right," Faye blurted. "I shouldn't pass judgment on someone I haven't met before. She's really pretty."

"Yeah," he said and smiled. "She is."

"So, what's your plan? Are you going to ask her out? You're not seriously considering signing up for something in the next rodeo, are you?"

Adam shrugged. "I suppose that all depends on how well you can teach me."

For what felt like a solid minute, she thought he was serious. But then that tell-tale sign of his lips pulling into that adorable, crooked grin gave him away. She nudged him. "Don't *do* that."

"What? Don't you have any faith in yourself?"

"Of course I do. But I still don't condone joining the *rodeo*. Do you even know how many people *die* from that sort of thing?"

He rolled his eyes. "Do you know how many people die just crossing the street? Besides, I'd rather go out doing something worthwhile than sitting at home twiddling my thumbs, wishing for something to change."

While his perspective was admirable, she couldn't bring herself to let him throw his life away. There were so many better options for getting a girl to fall for him. But there was no foreseeable way for her to change his mind. Her best shot would be to gain his respect first so he would take her advice later.

Faye pressed her lips together tightly. "Remember what I said about girls liking you for more than being a cowboy? Just think about that a little, okay?" If she couldn't get him to forget about competing by pointing out the danger, then maybe she could get him to see that shallow people like Dahlia weren't worth it.

His gaze bore into her, chipping away at her confidence and making her feel like a fool. What did she even know about love? She hadn't really dated anyone seriously. All she knew was what it meant to be a girl in this day and age. And she wouldn't want a guy to go risking anything just to impress her. Stupid stunts like that weren't attractive at all.

"Adam?"

They both turned toward the barista who held out two cups. Adam stepped forward to retrieve them then nodded toward the door. "Come on. Let's get back to the shop. We can start draining that oil."

The conversation was over. That was that. He wasn't interested in her giving him any advice when it came to love. And why would he be? They barely knew each other.

"Thanks," she murmured, taking the cup from his hand. Their fingertips brushed against one another, and it felt like a thousand butterflies flowed from his finger to hers and went right up to her heart. She jumped, staring at her hand. That was weird.

When she looked up, Adam was already pulling open the

door. She lengthened her stride to catch up to him, barely doing so before he got out onto the sidewalk.

"Hey," she puffed. "I'm sorry if I said something wrong back there."

He eyed her briefly. "You didn't do anything wrong."

"Then why do I get the feeling you're mad at me?"

"I'm not mad."

"You could have fooled me."

He stopped suddenly and faced her. "I'm not mad. But I do find it a little invasive—what you're doing. I don't understand why you even care."

She didn't get it herself. For all intents and purposes, she really should have just butted out. Why *was* she so interested in helping him?

"Well?"

Faye snapped up her head which was a grave mistake. Now she was caught in the snare of his gaze. If she didn't know any better, she would have thought he could read her mind—something she was already having a hard time trying to understand. Faye swallowed down the lump that had formed in her throat and shoved aside every irrational thought that continued to bubble to the surface.

"I don't want to see you get hurt."

He took a step closer to her, and her breath hitched in her chest. When his voice lowered to a husky level, she knew she was a goner. "Oh yeah? Why is that?"

"Because—I—if you die, who's going to fix my mom's truck?" Her voice wavered, breaking in weird places and making her sound like some poor unfortunate teenager.

What was happening to her?

The right side of Adam's face scrunched up. He tilted his head like a confused puppy. For a second there, she thought he would call her a liar. Mostly because that's exactly what she felt like. She wasn't being honest with him, but she wasn't quite being honest with herself either.

Adam lowered his face closer to her, and for reasons beyond her ken, she closed her eyes. His voice broke through the loud buzzing in her ears. "I'm not going to die before I fix your truck. I promise you that."

Her eyes fluttered open when she felt him shift in front of her.

He straightened, shoving his free hand into his pocket before he took a sip of his coffee. "And if you're going to make it a habit of offering your advice as it pertains to my love life, perhaps you should try to become my friend first." Adam brushed past her, whistling a familiar tune and leaving her behind, frozen in place.

It was as if her feet had grown roots and decided to plant themselves right there in the concrete. Her heart flitted madly in her chest. Her skin hummed with a strange kind of electricity. Every one of her senses screamed for her to hit the rewind button so she could enjoy that brief moment in slow motion.

"You coming?"

She jumped, spinning around. Adam was a few yards away, casually standing in the middle of the sidewalk as if he hadn't just caused the universe to shift and tilt on its side. Once again, she found herself asking the same question.

What was happening to her?

Faye had to be sick. That was the only logical explanation. She'd come down with something and she probably needed to just go home and take a nap.

But one look in Adam's direction, and she knew she'd hate herself for making such a decision. She wanted to investigate these new sensations that had awoken in her body. She needed to be near ground zero.

"Wait, did you say *friends*?" She walked toward him

cautiously so as not to give away just how excited this notion made her.

Adam shrugged, falling into step beside her. "Why not?"

There were several reasons. Wasn't there some unspoken rule that girls and guys couldn't be friends without making it incredibly complicated? Not only that, but she wasn't sure they would click. Friendships were supposed to happen organically.

In a small cloud of red smoke, that little version of herself appeared with a wicked smile, insisting that she deserved to have a little fun and that Adam was the first exciting person she'd interacted with since before she could remember.

Faye could feel his gaze on her as they continued walking. Every last drop of will she possessed went into not falling prey to his attention. She lifted a shoulder as nonchalantly as she could and brought the straw of her iced latte to her lips. "Sure. Why not? Friends, it is."

～

"*Ha!* You were wrong." Faye plopped onto Grace's bed, causing her sister to bounce with the inertia. "Adam has zero interest in me. He said so himself."

Those words were enough to garner Grace's attention. "He told you he wasn't interested in you?" Her voice dripped with disbelief. "Guys don't typically share that kind of information on their own..." Realization slapped her across the face. "Oh, Faye, please tell me you didn't."

"What? I didn't do anything!"

Grace put aside the book she'd been reading on the bed beside her. "You didn't ask him to confess anything? Or bring up the subject of your budding relationship?"

"Friendship," she corrected. "We've agreed to be friends."

Grace placed her palm on her forehead. "Why do I always feel like I'm the smart one in the family?"

"Maybe because you are." Faye sprawled on her back and stared at the ceiling. "We had fun doing some car stuff today, but before we got started, he wanted to get some coffee."

"Sounds like a date to me."

Faye craned her head around to give her sister a pointed look. "I told you. He's not interested. We even ran into the girl he's trying to impress. Now that was something you probably would have loved to see. He got all nervous like he was a little seventh grader asking his first crush to the dance or something. He couldn't even talk."

Grace still wore that look of doubt. It covered every square inch of her face, from the way her brows creased to her thinned lips.

"I'm *telling* you, Grace. Adam Cullen isn't interested in me. If he were, he'd get all tongue-tied and nervous. It was actually kinda cute if you think about it. Anyway, I told him I'd try to help him win her over. So that's that."

"I don't believe you."

"Yeah, I didn't think you would—mostly because you weren't there. But you'll see. When this whole arrangement is over and he wins the heart of the girl he wants, you'll be eating your words."

Grace drew her legs to her chest and wrapped her arms around them. "And what about you?"

"What about me?" Faye rolled over onto her stomach. She traced the stitching of the comforter with her finger absently, praying Grace didn't ask the one question Faye herself didn't know the answer to.

"Do you think there's a possibility that one day you won't want to help him find love with someone else? Perhaps you might want him to have eyes for you instead?"

Faye's heart reacted, constricting the blood flow and making it hard for her lungs to process the oxygen she needed. As a result, she choked a little.

Grace gave her a knowing smile. "See? I knew there was something—"

A groan escaped her chest and Faye sat up. "Of course there's a possibility that I would be attracted to him one day. That's a given. It's been scientifically proven, too, hasn't it?"

"I don't know."

"Well, just because it's a possibility doesn't mean that it will happen for sure. So how about you and Bri just drop it and let me do my thing the way I want to." She slid from the bed and headed for the door. This moment of triumph had been lessened by Grace's assumptions. For once, Faye had thought she'd have the upper hand, but in true Grace fashion, her sister had to ruin her moment.

She'd see—one day. Adam would choose Dahlia, and Faye would have... what exactly? Her truck?

Yep. Faye would have the truck her mother left them. And that would be enough.

8

———

Adam

 eekends were the only time Adam worked with Faye. His schedule was too full for anything else. The funny thing was that he found himself looking forward to seeing her even after their strange interaction the previous week.

It had taken almost a full week to work through the aches from his last encounter with Blaze, but driving onto the Callahan property caused all his muscles to tighten again. He got out of his truck, then glanced once at the house, wondering if he should knock or just wait for her to appear.

Neither of those options sounded great at the moment, so instead, Adam headed for the barn. Faye would materialize at some point. Until then he would wait with the animals.

The air was humid and the clouds overhead cast the whole property in an almost gray hue. The boots Adam wore sunk into the soft earth beneath him. With each step, the scent of fresh rain, pine, and earth seemed to erupt into the air.

Adam breathed in deeply. There was something about living out here in the country. Yes, he lived in Copper Creek too, but it was different out here, surrounded by barns, corrals, and rolling hills. While the town portion of Copper Creek was small, it was still more congested than the surrounding ranches.

He stepped into the barn only to find his teacher was already there. Not only that, but she had both horses saddled and was waiting for him. Faye leaned against the stalls to the right, her ankles and arms crossed. The light coming from the other side of the building only accentuated her silhouette. She wore a hat and jacket along with her usual western wear.

Faye's head lifted as he approached. What should have been just a normal meeting was, in fact, not. Normally he saddled his own horse and they did exercises. Something just felt different. She pushed away from the stall with a smile on her face. "You're gonna love today." Then with a flourish, she pulled open the stall where Blaze was ready and waiting. "We're going for a ride."

"A *real* ride? Like out on a trail or something?"

"Of course."

"But don't I need a little more practice? I thought last time —" His heart stuttered, but he couldn't tell if it was due to his anxiety over being thrown last time or if it was the way her warm hand brushed against his when she pressed the reins to his palm.

"Don't worry. I won't go any faster than you're ready for."

"Yeah, what about *him*?" Adam motioned toward Blaze. "Are you going to make me ride him again? Or do I get to try with Bella?"

She placed a hand on her hip as it popped to the side and

made her look even more alluring. "You're not *afraid,* are you? If you're going to make Dahlia give you a second look, you're gonna have to get past that."

Oh, *right*. Dahlia. That's what this was about. One riding lesson and one car session, and already he'd shifted his sights to the girl who stood in front of him rather than the one who he'd pined over for the past several weeks.

Faye's soft laugh broke past his defenses. It managed to invade where others had failed. How could something so small and simple cause so many sensations? She brushed past him, leading a different horse he hadn't seen before. It was almost completely white and could have passed for a knight's faithful steed in any number of fairytales.

When she reached the edge of the barn, she paused and glanced over her shoulder. "Are you coming or not? I've got something to show you."

For a moment he froze. It was as if his feet didn't have any idea of what to do next. They remained glued to the spot until he heard that laughter again. It echoed off the walls, wrapping around him and making him lurch forward so as not to get left behind.

Adam's long stride had him easily catching up to Faye, and just when he got to her side, she lifted herself up into the saddle. Behind her a flicker of light caught his attention. He nodded toward the lightning. "Are you sure we should be riding? It looks like it's gonna rain again."

She followed his gesture and then swung her attention back to him. "Don't tell me you're scared of rain, too."

"I'm not *scared*," he muttered indignantly. "I just don't know that we should be taking the horses out in it. Isn't it bad for them?"

"First of all, that storm is a far way off. Second, *if* we get rained on, we can dry them up just fine when we get back.

This is important. We won't go riding for another two weeks. Come on. Get in the saddle like you did last time." She pulled her reins around and moved her horse forward without even waiting for him.

Adam scrambled around to Blaze's left side and mounted with little effort. There was only a faint ache in his legs, but that could have been from anything. He was just about to dig his heels into Blaze's sides when he recalled how that worked out for him last time. Instead, he carefully squeezed his legs and the horse moved forward.

Much better.

Blaze was far more sensitive than Adam had realized. The horse could move in one direction or the other with a simple shift in the saddle. He appeared to be able to sense where Adam wanted to go before he was prompted. And it was absolutely amazing.

Growing a little more confident with every step, Adam nudged Blaze into a quicker pace.

Big mistake.

Blaze moved into a trot that was a decent speed, but the way Adam was seated, his backside bore the brunt of every clip-clop Blaze took. The pain returned with a vengeance, reminding Adam he wasn't a young teenager anymore.

He was just about to pull on the reins to slow down when Faye's laughter pulled his attention. She shook her head but didn't say anything.

"Are you going to do your job or what?" Wasn't she supposed to give him advice or tips on how to stay in the saddle without losing all feeling in his rump? This didn't feel right. And if it was, the folks in all those movies and television shows made it seem so much easier.

Faye eyed him. "But it's so entertaining watching your process."

"What process? The 'I'll do it wrong until I get knocked to the ground' process?"

She laughed again and he couldn't help but join in with her. He tugged briefly on the reins, and Blaze slowed to a walk so they were riding side by side. Faye shifted in her saddle and stared straight ahead. "What is it you want me to teach you exactly?"

"How to ride without getting hurt would be nice."

A grin tugged at her lips. "Seems you're catching on just fine. You got Blaze to slow down without finding his eject button."

"Funny," he drawled.

"*I* thought so." She peeked at him so briefly he wasn't sure she'd actually done it.

His hands gripped the leather reins tighter. "Let's start with riding faster and not bruising my tailbone in the process. Can you tell me what I'm doing wrong?" He turned toward her, allowing himself to study her a little more. When he'd first met her, he would have considered her average. But that was before he'd heard her laugh and before he'd started to get to know her.

Faye had managed to catch his attention in more ways than one. She wasn't conventionally attractive like he'd found Dahlia. He hadn't been immediately drawn to her. But she was pretty. She had freckles across her nose, and her blonde hair seemed to change hue based on the kind of sunlight that shone on it. She was strong as was proven by her ability to handle horses and their saddles. She talked a little too much and laughed even more, though he couldn't help but love the latter.

"You okay?"

He jumped. "What?"

Faye's hand was in front of her, palm outward as if she'd

been waving at him. She dropped it and let it dangle at her side as her eyes narrowed. "I said you're not sitting in the saddle right."

"There's a wrong way to sit in the saddle?"

"Isn't there a wrong way to take apart a car?"

He scoffed. "Those two things are nothing alike."

"Fair enough." She faced forward once more, showing him her profile. "When you're riding, there are rules you have to follow, though. Like when I taught you to mount on the left side."

"Okay, I can see that. What rules are you referring to?"

"You should hold your reins with a soft hand. Too tight and you'll get bucked. Too loose and depending on the horse, they could stop listening to you." Her gaze dipped to Blaze. "He wouldn't do that. He's one of the best there is. Aren't you, Blaze?"

The horse tossed his head back, nickering.

"Okay, so hold the reins with a firm and gentle hand. What else?"

"You already know not to kick too hard. But you also want to make sure you're not squeezing your legs too tight. And when you're riding at faster speeds, you want to move with your horse."

Adam snickered. "I didn't think I *could* move without him."

"No, you misunderstand. It's almost like a dance. You need to put your weight on the stirrups so when the horse comes up, you don't come down. Like I said, you have to follow the momentum so you're both up and down at the same time. Then you won't feel like you're about to be jostled from the saddle."

What she said actually made some sense. He'd have to remember to try it the next time he had feeling in his legs. At this point, they were getting that tingling sensation again. "So where are we going? What's so special out here that you couldn't wait until we had a sunnier day?"

That's when her features brightened enough to rival the sun itself. Her eyes lit up like two shining stars and her smile had him wishing it would never fade.

"There are mountains and hills all over this valley that are amazing to see when the sun rises or sets. But there is only one place I can think of that looks the best after the rain."

"Yeah? Where's that?"

Without warning, she let out a "Hyah!" and urged her horse forward.

There was a moment between the second she left and Blaze taking off when he wondered if he might lose her.

He shouldn't have been worried at all.

Blaze took off like a shot, running with a smooth, even gait. It was so much easier to stay in the saddle and blend his body with the animal. The only experience that even came close to this one was that time he got to test drive a vintage sports car at a show.

His spirit had become one with Blaze, and together they chased down the girl whose laughter was all it took to make his heart trip over itself.

Adam lost track of how long they rode. It could have been ten minutes or an hour. The scenery blurred around them into shades of green and blue as they left the fenced area behind and charged onto a trail that led them straight for the crevice between two steep hills.

Up, up, up they climbed past bushes, rocks and wildflowers into thicker trees and steeper trails. Out of nowhere a babbling brook cascaded parallel to the trail, its dull blue coloring reflecting the sky overhead.

Then finally, they came to a stop.

The landscape that surrounded him felt like a small slice

of heaven. Trees rose around him, blocking his view of the ranch or the rest of the woods. It took a few minutes to get his bearings and when he did, he finally realized why Faye brought him up here.

The brook widened toward the edge of the clearing. No longer was it babbling. Now it was thrashing over rocks and under a fallen tree.

Faye slipped from her saddle gracefully and took a few steps in that direction before she stopped and looked at him. "Well?"

"Well, what?"

"Aren't you coming?"

His focus bounced from her to the water's edge. "What are we going to do? I didn't bring a swimming suit."

This time her laugh wasn't soft, meek, or teasing. Nope. This time, she'd tossed back her head and hooted. "That little pond is nowhere big enough for either of us to go swimming in. It's what's just beyond it that you'll want to see." She spun around and charged toward the water.

Adam scrambled from his saddle and hurried over to her, only to skid to a stop before nearly leaping off the edge of a steep drop-off. Water came up just below the top of his boots, some of it splashing onto his pants. The view had been very deceiving. The water was flowing toward the cliff, and it fell down several hundred feet to the base of the mountain they'd just ridden up.

He let out a low whistle.

Faye nudged him in the ribs with her elbow. "See? I told you this was great."

"Yeah, but you have yet to tell me why we came up this way. This is cool and everything, but—"

"It's the perfect place for a date, don't you think?"

His words caught in his throat. Was she suggesting they

were on a date right now? That was the only explanation that made sense in his head. She'd insisted on taking a ride when a visit to the corral would have sufficed. Now they stood at the top of the world alone, and she wanted to show him something that was important to her.

Adam glanced at her. Surprisingly, he didn't see anything wrong with that idea. Perhaps he'd been too focused on Dahlia when Faye standing right there in front of him.

She turned her beautiful smile to him and gestured around them. "Don't you think this place is romantic? You could put a picnic blanket there with candles and a bottle of champagne. You could ride up here for a night of star gazing. Dahlia would be super impressed if you brought her up here."

That's when his stomach bottomed out.

He'd misunderstood, and the disappointment that started in his gut had made its way into his throat. The sour taste was a reminder that he needed to keep his eye on the prize.

Unfortunately, Faye didn't fit into that plan.

9

Faye

"I know you're probably not even thinking that far ahead, but seriously, this is the most romantic place I've ever been." She wrapped her arms around herself. If she wasn't careful, Adam would pity her for these silly daydreams. Faye glanced at him, finding him studying her, and her cheeks immediately flushed. "What?"

"Let me guess, your boyfriend brought you here or vice versa."

She looked away. "Nope."

"Which one?"

"Both."

He was silent, and she could just imagine what he was thinking. Poor Faye Callahan, who had never dated. It could be worse. He might even think he shouldn't be listening to her advice because she had no experience.

Well, if that was what he thought, he was wrong. What she

had to say held value because she was a girl and she knew what a girl would like. She gestured around them. "I wanted to show you this place, and I thought we could make a few trips out here so you don't get lost when you eventually bring Dahlia here."

"Who says I'm going to bring Dahlia out here?" His wry smile said it all. He didn't trust her advice.

"Because if you're serious about this girl, you'll do something to show her you like her. Could you take her to dinner and a movie, and then maybe a stroll down Main Street? Of course you could. But how many other guys do you think have done exactly that?"

His smug look faded. There. He was catching on.

"Do you know how often a girl fantasizes about coming to a place like this just to talk or share a picnic? Girls like romance. They like to be swept off their feet. You have to figure out what she likes and do it. Based on what you've told me, I just figured she'd like this place because she likes to go riding. But you could come up with something else if you want." She was rambling and she knew it. Why couldn't she just say her piece and be done with it?

In an attempt to stop sounding so pathetic, she surveyed the area she'd picked out. This place was like heaven. As embarrassing as it was to admit, she'd fantasized about coming here just like she'd told him. Eventually, she realized that there wasn't a guy in Copper Creek who would ever bring her here, and it wasn't just because none of them knew about it. No one seemed to have an interest in her, whether because of her father or her own personality. It didn't *really* bother her. Faye had always managed to find happiness despite her disappointments.

She snuck a glance in his direction, finding Adam scanning the area again. His expression softened and he nodded.

"Okay. I can see it. Are you sure your dad would be okay with me bringing someone here?"

"Sure. Why not?"

He gave her a pointed look, and she laughed.

"Okay, so I'll have to tell him that I gave you permission to borrow our horses and that you'd be wandering the property." She grimaced. "Actually, he probably wouldn't want you to come out here on your own unless you've taken a few trips. So maybe we can come up with a way for you to be guided here."

He made a face. "If I'm supposed to have a romantic picnic or outing or whatever, I'm not going to want to have a chaperone. That sort of defeats the purpose, doesn't it?"

"Then I guess we'll have to take more rides out this way. Maybe after a few, you can be the one to guide the way."

He looked thoughtful on that one. Before he had a chance to say anything, a rumble overhead shattered the serene overcast afternoon. Adam jumped and his eyes grew wide. He shot a disgruntled look in her direction. "I told you we shouldn't be out here."

Faye didn't know why she found this so amusing, but she did. She let out a small laugh. "A little rain never hurt anyone."

The thunder clapped again and Adam flinched. It hadn't started raining yet, so it was just the sound that he didn't seem to like. He ducked down when it boomed then shook his head. "What if lightning strikes? What about the horses? Don't they hate this sort of thing?"

Faint flickering light rippled through the clouds overhead. Faye was one of those people who actually liked storms. She didn't care if she was out in the rain or safely tucked away in a shelter—thunderstorms were her favorite.

She tilted her face to the sky and closed her eyes, loving the smell of the humidity in the air. There was only a slight electrical current that seemed to hover over them. This storm was mild compared to some of the others she'd been in.

One large, fat drop of water splashed on her cheek like a missile seeking out its target. The impact caused that droplet to explode into several smaller ones. Faye smiled as she waited for the next one and the next.

He was watching her. She could feel it without even looking at him. Those serious eyes of his were probably judging her right at this very moment. Well, she wasn't going to let him take this away from her. It had been a while since she'd been able to revel beneath the rush of raindrops that would soon wash over them.

"Shouldn't we start heading back?" His voice was hesitant.

"Are you really that nervous?" Her chin dropped down and she stared at him with a teasing smile. "When was the last time you had a little fun? Have you ever just enjoyed the rain before?"

"Yes," he countered.

She gave him a pointed look. Based on everything he had said since the start of their ride, she had a hard time believing that.

Adam squirmed beneath her stare. Then he sighed and dragged his hand down his face. "I just prefer enjoying my storms from the safety of my home. Behind a pane of glass."

"You're no fun."

Raindrops were falling faster now. They were small and scattered all over, thudding against the ground and the blades of grass with soft sounds. They wouldn't do much damage to their clothing unless they got larger.

As if her thoughts alone were the driving force for this storm, the rain suddenly fell from the sky in sheets.

Adam let out a curse and ducked, though there was nowhere for him to go. He held his hands over his head and gave her a dirty look. Lightning flashed, filling the sky with a bright, hot light. Thunder cracked, splitting the sky in two. The horse that Faye had ridden up here reared back on her hind legs and charged out of the clearing.

Adam's mouth dropped open, his hands still holding tight to Blaze's reins. "Is she going to be okay?" he hollered, blinking rapidly and then wiping the water from his face.

Faye nodded. She had to squint her eyes to see through the downpour. "She knows her way back. But we should probably head back."

"You *think*?" His tone was sharper than it had been since she'd met him.

"You really don't like the rain, do you?"

"This isn't rain. This is Noah's next flood."

She couldn't help but laugh even though her clothes were saturated and her horse had disappeared. The hair that wasn't covered by her hat hung limply around her shoulders as rivulets of water trailed down the ends. "It will pass. We probably won't get back before it does. You might as well enjoy it."

He gave her a dumbfounded look. "Seriously?" His focus shifted to Blaze. "How are we even going to head back? We only have one horse."

"You could walk." Faye said it without humor, though she didn't mean a word of it. Adam needed to lighten up. Where was the easygoing guy she'd been working with? It didn't take any effort at all for his attitude to shift when he just got a little wet.

Okay, that wasn't fair. He was drenched just like she was, and the storm actually didn't look like it would be moving out any time soon.

The look Adam gave her was absolutely priceless. He gaped at her, presumably unaware of the water at this point.

She couldn't take it. A laugh erupted from her throat and she shook her head. "You make it too easy. We'll both ride Blaze back and I'll make sure we hurry. Don't worry. You can use the stirrups. Come on. Let's get going." Faye trudged toward him and motioned for him to get on the horse first. Then she nudged his leg. "I still need the stirrup to get into the saddle. Move back as far as you can if you don't want to get my boot in your face."

In one easy movement, she climbed up onto the front of the saddle and scooted as far forward as she could. Adam readjusted himself onto the saddle. She could sense just how stiff he was, seated behind her. He wasn't holding onto anything, and there was no way he'd stay on the horse if they were going to move fast.

Faye twisted in her seat and gave him a look. "I'm not going to bite. Go ahead and hold onto me. I'd rather you not fall off the horse this time."

His lips quirked up at the ends. "So you admit you wanted me to fall last time?"

Biting back a smile, Faye faced forward. "No comment."

Blaze shuffled restlessly beneath them. He might be a better-trained horse, but he still didn't like the storm. She should have gone home sooner just for him, but she'd been enjoying herself with Adam too much.

Faye leaned forward, patting his neck. "Okay, buddy, get us home nice and safe and I'll make sure you get extra sweets tonight."

He tossed his head as if he understood every single word she'd said to him. She grinned before glancing back at Adam. "I mean it. Hold onto me. He's gonna go fast."

Adam grasped her waist limply, and she rolled her eyes. He'd learn the second Blaze took off. Faye dug her heels inward and Blaze shot forward. Adam's hands tightened immediately, and she nearly lost her own balance to even out the weight distribution they had in the saddle.

Dirt flew up around them as Blaze's hooves thundered against the wet ground. They darted along the trail, heading back the way they'd come. Slowly, Adam's stiff form relaxed, but she couldn't tell if it was because he was comfortable now or if it was for self-preservation. The warmth of his body against her broke through their wet clothes and flooded her with a strange sensation. Electrified flutters ripped along every nerve ending. She nearly jerked away from him, but that would have been problematic seeing as they were still running along the trails to head home.

Instead, she forced herself to focus on the path before them. Don't fall from the horse. Don't let Adam fall from the horse. Just get back in one piece.

And whatever she did, she needed to avoid thinking of the way it felt being held by him. Going down that rabbit hole wouldn't do either of them any good. He already had his sights set on someone else. And that wasn't her.

The more those thoughts cycled through her mind, the more her mood worsened. She'd never been the kind of person who pitied herself. There was never a reason to feel that way. Even now, she battled with that idea. What did she have to feel bad about? She hadn't gone into this arrangement to find love. She wanted her mother's truck fixed. She was getting exactly what she wanted.

When her family home and barn came into view, she pushed Blaze a little harder. The sooner she could get out of this saddle and put some distance between herself and Adam, the better.

Faye pulled up hard on the reins, harder than she'd meant to, causing Blaze to do what he was known to do. He pulled up on his hind legs. It wasn't as high as it had been when Adam had experienced it last time and neither one of them fell from the saddle, but it did cause Adam to cling to her harder.

She scrambled from the saddle abruptly and immediately pulled the reins around to lead Blaze to shelter. Adam didn't have a chance to climb down until they were out of the rain. Not surprising, their other horse had returned and was standing aimlessly in the middle of the barn, still saddled. It didn't look like anyone had taken notice of her arrival, which was just as well because Faye needed an excuse to stay busy.

Their ride was over, she'd humiliated herself, and now she was having these feelings that wouldn't go away despite the logic she threw at them.

Adam dismounted and hovered as she set to work. If he'd said anything, she hadn't paid attention. She removed the saddles and dried off both horses after putting them in their stalls. Then she placed a cooling rug on them to help wick away the moisture. This was all done as if she were on autopilot, and she nearly forgot that Adam was there.

Until he tapped her on the shoulder.

Faye nearly screamed as she spun around and stumbled back against the stall wall. She covered her mouth with her hand and let out a strangled laugh. "I'm sorry."

He tilted his head, his gaze drilling into her. "What for? I should be the one to apologize. You've done all the work and I've just sat back and let you."

She glanced from him to the horses. "Honestly? Sometimes I just get in the zone and do all the work without thinking. Besides, this part isn't really something you'd need to learn."

Adam was only a few inches from her, and with the wood to her back, she suddenly felt cornered. But she refused to move or give any indication that something was amiss. He pointed to Blaze, who was in the stall behind her. "Why did you put that on him?"

Faye glanced back once more. "That's a cooling rug. Depending on the workout or the conditions of the workout, you pick one of a certain weight or material. It helps him regulate his body temperature."

"Oh." He didn't move. His gaze seemed to be searching hers. Even though they weren't touching, she could feel the heat radiating from him. Or maybe that was in her imagination. Of course, it could just be due to her own chilled body temperature since being out in the rain.

She swallowed hard, her hands pressing against the wall at her back. "I guess we're done today unless you have any other questions..."

"Are *you* done?"

"No."

Surprise flitted across his face, but she didn't know why. "Don't tell me you're going to go riding again today?"

A smile broke across her face, and she shook her head. "I've got to take care of the tack. Leather and water don't do well together. But you're free to leave—"

"I think I'll stay if that's okay."

10

———

Adam

*A*dam probably shouldn't have said that. He should just go like she asked.

She *did* ask, didn't she? Faye wanted to get to work. It was clear by the way she just went all robotic that she didn't want him there. It was like watching a well-oiled machine. The way she took care of the horses after their ride was almost mesmerizing. He should have spoken up at that point. He could have helped.

But something held him back, and he didn't know what it was exactly.

"You want to *stay*." Her voice was laced with an almost judgmental tone. Or disbelief. It was entirely possible that was what she was feeling.

Well, why wouldn't he stay? He was teaching her how to fix a truck in a way. Why wouldn't he want to learn what it takes to handle a horse? What if he wanted to purchase one?

Oh yeah, she was staring at him.

Adam chuckled and shrugged. "Sure. I could help. I detail enough cars. Saddles shouldn't be too different, right?"

Her brows pulled together, smile gone. She was close enough to touch, and he itched to brush away a strand of wet hair that clung to the hollow of her neck. But that would be too forward. He couldn't just touch her like that.

Right?

Yes, most definitely. Touching her would be inappropriate.

"Just tell me what I can do to help. Then I'll take us to get some coffee."

"You want to get some coffee?" Her voice cracked and those eyes of hers continued to penetrate him right to his soul. He needed to leave. She'd asked him to. He should just go. So why couldn't he take the steps backward, bid her farewell, and tell her he'd see her in a week?

Because, the truth was, a week was beginning to feel like an eternity and he wanted to get to know her a little more. These short sessions weren't nearly long enough.

Adam let out a heavy sigh. "Fine, if you don't want to—"

"No. I'll go." She looked away, her long lashes brushing against her cheeks. Then her hand came up and brushed away that strand of hair that had caught his attention in the first place. "I mean, I'd never turn down a free cup of coffee." Her lashes fluttered and she glanced up at him once more.

He didn't know what prompted him to take a step closer, but he did. The distance between them shrank and the electrical current intensified much like the storm they'd just escaped from. Her gaze was locked with his, and it was like he'd lost all control of his ability to think clearly.

Something clattered toward the entrance of the barn, and they both jumped. One of the ranch hands picked up a pitchfork that had fallen to the floor. He waved toward them and then grabbed another tool and disappeared.

When Adam turned his attention to Faye, she brushed past him, all business again. "Tack is important to keep dry. If you're out riding in the rain, you need to take care of it as soon as the horse has been helped. Leaving it to the next day isn't an option if you don't want to be out several hundred dollars."

Yep. All business.

That was fine.

Faye was the kind of person who could mesmerize her audience purely by the way she stayed on task. She had a talent with everything in this barn she touched. From the way she could clean and lubricate the saddle and bridles they'd used to the way she inspected every loop and buckle. She talked fast, and he wasn't ashamed to say he enjoyed just listening to her as he watched her work.

She stopped suddenly and faced him. "I just realized I'm doing all the work again."

He stiffened. Was that a comment meant to put him in his place? He'd offered to help, after all.

Her cheeks colored and she laced her fingers behind her neck. "I'm sorry. I know you're not gonna be able to learn a single thing by watching. Do you want to—"

Adam stepped forward and nodded. "What do you need me to do?"

She held out a small tin can. "Do you think you can handle the conditioner? After all, it's just like the interior of a car, right?" Faye's lips twitched upward, and he matched her grin with one of his own.

"Right."

Their fingertips grazed against one another, causing another spark to take place between them. Or maybe that was all in his head. Then again, it could be the storm and the way their boots scuffed against the floor in the barn.

She moved out of the way to give him space as he set to work. "Can I ask you a question?" she asked.

"Sure."

"Did you always want to work on cars?"

He stilled. No one had asked him that question as far as he could remember. Out of his brothers, he was the only one who'd taken a shine to the work his father did. None of them wanted anything to do with being a mechanic. Adam glanced at her out of the corner of his eye, and then he turned back to the task at hand. "Actually, no. I kinda fought it for a long time."

"Really."

He nodded. "But that was probably because my brothers did too. None of them wanted to be a mechanic. They thought they were better than that sort of work. I guess I sorta believed them."

"Did any of them become mechanics?"

He chuckled. "Nope. They all got jobs doing other stuff."

"But not you."

Adam shook his head. "It wasn't for lack of trying. When I left town to go to school, I wanted to do something—anything else. But the funny thing was that I realized I was actually really good at it. I could sense what was wrong with the cars that I worked on. First, I was just helping my friends with their own beat-up cars in college, then I turned it into a gig I did on the weekends. In the end, I realized I should just accept that this was what God had in store for me."

She hovered so close he could hear her soft breathing. He didn't dare look at her. He had no idea how she'd react. Here was this woman who was raised in the Callahan family, and she probably had the strongest family values of anyone this side of the Colorado River. It could go either way.

What if she looked down on him for not wanting to follow in his father's footsteps? On the other hand, she could judge him for coming back like the prodigal son he was. There was no telling what she was thinking, especially with how quiet she was being in that very moment.

"Sometimes I wonder if I should do what some of my sisters have done."

His hands stilled, no longer conditioning the saddle. "What do you mean?"

"You know, Like Constance, Dianna, and Grace."

Adam faced her. "You realize that the only one I know is Grace, right?"

She rolled her eyes. "My oldest sisters are the ones taking care of the ranch the way my father will need them to when he decides to retire. The rest of us have to figure out if we're going to hang around to help out or if we're going to go our own way. Grace is helping out at that Equine Therapy Center. She's my younger sister, and she's already found what she wants. And I'm..." She shrugged. "I'm just stuck. It's kinda embarrassing, you know?"

"You're helping *me*."

She gave him an irritated look. "We're trading services. That's not me helping anyone."

"Well, you're really good at it if that's any consolation. You've got a knack for explaining things that other people don't. What if you taught people how to ride?"

Faye's features blanked. Was that a good thing? Or had he offended her? He couldn't tell.

"Seriously. I've had a total of two lessons from you and—" he started but she interrupted.

"Right. The first one, you were bucked from your horse.

And the second, you had to double-up to ride through the rain. I wouldn't say you've had a very good track record. Or rather, I've not had a very good track record."

She made a good point, but that wasn't what he was dwelling on. Sure, he'd learned a lot from these two lessons. But more than that, he'd actually enjoyed himself, and that had everything to do with a certain someone who stood beside him.

Adam turned to face her fully. "I get that you're not feeling very confident right now but believe me when I tell you that I wouldn't mind paying for the kind of expertise I know you offer."

Faye rolled her lips together before pulling them into a small smile. "Thanks, Adam."

"Don't mention it." Adam wasn't the type of person to give compliments. But that didn't mean he wasn't willing to tell the truth. Faye was obviously knowledgeable when it came to horsemanship. She knew how to put things in simple terms to aid in the learning process. And she was humble enough to brush off something she didn't believe to be true.

He stepped back to admire his work. "How about that?"

She moved in closer and her shoulder brushed against his. Faye smelled like the rain outside and a faint floral scent. There were other notes of something he couldn't place, but he found that the combination of all of it was nothing like he'd ever experienced before. He was usually in a garage with the smell of oil and other chemicals they used for the vehicles they worked on.

Faye was a breath of fresh air—literally. It took all his self-control not to lean in and breathe deeply. She turned her chin over her shoulder and smiled at him. "This looks great. I'm impressed."

Adam smiled, lifting his shoulders. "I told you. I have a lot of experience with detailing leather seats in the cars I work on. This was nothing."

She rolled her eyes. "Glad to see your experience hasn't given you a big head." Faye spun on her heel and brushed past him again. Each time her body made contact with his, a strange sensation occurred. It was enough to draw his attention and make him do a double take. His gut twisted in an unsettling way and he couldn't drag his focus from her as she headed off toward the door.

He charged after her. "Are we done then? Does this mean we can go get that coffee to warm up?"

Faye stopped suddenly and spun around. Her amused expression was the first thing he noticed before her gaze swept over him from head to toe. "You're soaked to the bone. Aren't you going to want to head home to change before going out?"

She was right to a degree. His clothes had already started to dry a little. That didn't mean they weren't rubbing his skin raw underneath the surface, though. He might be able to grab a spare change of clothes at the auto shop.

Only he didn't want to do that either. For some strange reason, he didn't want to leave her here. It was as if the act of doing so would result in her not being willing to come with him. It was a lot easier for him to get her to agree when he was standing in front of her.

Adam shifted under her gaze and let out a dry chuckle. "I'm sure I can find something at the shop on the way to Sal's. You can go ahead and change, though, and I'll wait in my truck." For a second, he wasn't sure if she was going to follow through with their... what was it? A date? That didn't sound right, though he couldn't deny the thought of taking her on a date gave him its own kind of thrill.

She tilted her head, watching him for a moment before she shrugged. "You can get me coffee if you'd like, but I'm going to get myself some pie. I haven't had a good slice of Sal's apple pie in ages." They stood at the edge of the barn, the sound of the rain hitting the earth being the only thing that filled the void.

"They still make that there?"

Faye nodded. "How long did you say you've been back in town?"

He gave her a chagrined smile. "A couple months, but I haven't had a chance to really go out anywhere."

Her pointed look said it all and was enough to make his stomach drop. "Except to the rodeo."

"Yeah. I guess that's where I've been spending most of my time."

She glanced out toward the rain and grimaced. "Is it ridiculous that I don't want to go out into the rain right now?"

"Who's scared of the rain now?"

"I'm not scared of the rain. I'm just getting comfortable." Even as she said the words, she shivered. It wasn't any wonder that she'd prefer to stay sheltered. Faye sighed. "But that pie sounds *so* good."

He stood there for a moment, the urge to do something truly reckless hovering in the back of his mind. Something held him back, but he wasn't quite sure what it was. To heck with it. He wasn't going to be a slave to these feelings that told him to be cautious. When did that ever get him anywhere?

In one swift movement, Adam scooped Faye into his arms and darted out into the rain. At first she screamed, her arms wrapping tight around his neck as she clung to him. He let out a laugh as he ran toward the house and waves of rain poured over them. It didn't feel as cold as it had when they'd been riding. It was almost warm despite it being spring.

Faye's arms relaxed and she tilted her face toward the rain for a moment before she glanced at him.

Shoot.

She'd caught him staring.

Again.

Their eyes locked for only a moment because that was how quickly he arrived at the house. He deposited her onto the porch and took a swift step back. "There. Now you're here, and you're not as wet as you might have been." He jerked his thumb over his shoulder. "I'm getting in the truck. Come on out when you're ready to go. I'm not in a hurry."

He couldn't get to his vehicle fast enough. He shouldn't have done that. Whatever she was probably thinking of him wasn't going to be very good. The second she got in the truck, she was probably going to put him in his place.

Even as these thoughts dragged him down, one thought rose above them all.

It was totally worth it.

11

____

Faye

Faye stuck her fork into her pie. She couldn't bring herself to look Adam in the eye because she knew if she did, he'd probably see just how much she was starting to like him. They hadn't discussed the way he'd lifted her up like she weighed nothing at all. That didn't stop her from thinking about how it had made her feel to be wrapped up in his strong arms.

Okay, thoughts like that were only going to get her in trouble. How many times had she seen that happen? People who developed feelings for someone who would never return said feelings always ended up hurt.

She couldn't allow that to happen.

She wouldn't.

Faye took another bite of her pie as her annoying thoughts continued bouncing around in her head like a lost rubber ball. Maybe she shouldn't be so stiff. What would happen if she actually opened herself up to being closer to him? It wasn't like she could avoid him. They had that agreement, and she didn't know how long it would really last.

Her eyes darted up to find him staring at her and she froze. From the way her heart refused to beat to the way her lungs went rigid, she'd be lucky if she didn't pass out right here, right now.

Adam looked concerned more than anything. His gaze didn't waver as his hands turned the mug around in his hands. His jaw was tight, too. This had to be the most awkward meal she had ever had.

Faye pointed to her pie with her fork, swallowing what she had in her mouth. "You want a bite?"

She'd expected him to turn her down—laugh, maybe. But he didn't. His focus shifted to the pie and he pulled it closer. Her voice died in her throat as she watched him with surprise. He grabbed the fork from her hand, stuck it in the pie and pulled a piece up to his mouth.

His brows lifted and he nodded. "You're right. That's pretty good." Adam pushed the pie back to her. "You gonna talk about what happened? Or do I have to bring it up?"

Faye would have choked if she had food in her mouth. Her whole body flinched, and she had to force herself to look up at him. "What are you talking about?"

"Are we going to talk about why you're so quiet?"

"Am I?"

He settled back in his seat and rolled his eyes. "Come on, Faye. I had expected you would bring it up when you climbed into my truck. But now we've been here for going on thirty minutes and you haven't said more than twelve words to me."

"I'm *eating*. Excuse me if I don't want to talk with my mouth full. You wouldn't be so thrilled about me speaking if you were getting bits of pie on your face."

His lips twitched but didn't fully form a smile. "Admit it. I took things too far when I lifted you up in the barn."

She didn't respond right away. He'd be able to tell if she was lying. And she hadn't been upset about the action at all. Should she have been?

Of course she should have been upset. He'd picked her up without asking her. But for some reason she couldn't bring herself to experience those emotions. It was probably because she felt safe with him. But the whole thing had been somewhat thrilling. In that moment, she'd been able to pretend that they were something more than they really were, even if it was just the start of something more.

Faye shrugged. "I'm not upset."

"I didn't say you were upset. I said that you think I went too far."

She took another bite of her pie, savoring the taste in her mouth. Maybe if she didn't respond, he would drop it.

"So?"

"Are you trying to get me to say I agree with you?" Ooh, that was not the route she should have taken.

"That's exactly what I'm saying."

"Well, if I had hurt my ankle, would you have carried me to the house?"

"Sure."

She pointed her fork at him again. "Okay, so if you would carry me in that situation and it wouldn't be a big deal, then it shouldn't matter in this case either." The argument was a weak one, and she knew it. The longer they talked about it, the more difficult it was to continue.

"That's different, and you know it."

Faye shrugged. "Did you surprise me? Yes. Was carrying me to my front porch necessary? No. Who cares?" She focused on her plate due to the pie being completely gone. There was nothing left to say. Why was he pushing this so hard? Faye placed her fork on the table and heaved a sigh. "What's the big deal? Did I weigh more than you thought I would or something? Did I forget to put on deodorant this morning?"

He stiffened and his eyes widened slightly. "What? No."

"Then let's just drop it. I'm not upset. And if it's bothering you so much, then just don't do it again, okay?"

"Fine."

Finally. Except now that the argument was over, she was left with that residual awkwardness that she couldn't shake. He was still staring at her, and they were both probably wondering why they had that conversation in the first place.

Faye turned her face toward the window and the dreary scene outside. She rubbed her hand on the back of her neck before finally glancing at Adam. "So why did you come back to town?"

He didn't react right away. Had she asked something wrong? Great. Here they went again.

Adam picked up one of the shriveled straw wrappers on the table and fiddled with it. "I told you. I'm good at being a mechanic. So I came to work for my dad."

Her eyes narrowed and she nibbled on her lower lip. "See? That doesn't make much sense to me. If you were doing so well—wherever you were living—why did you come back here? This place doesn't exactly give off *those* kinds of vibes."

Oh no. That small smile he wore was the exact thing that made her resolve crumble.

Adam crossed his arms, his brows furrowing. "What vibes are you talking about?"

"I don't know. Weren't you living in the city? I'm sure you get a lot more work out there."

He snorted. "Is that what you think? That I got a lot of work out there? Well, I'll have you know that I get a lot more work out here. Do you realize how many cowboys own farming equipment and trucks? And who do they take their stuff to? That's right. Me."

"Well, it's nice to know that you're not getting full of yourself." Faye rolled her eyes. "But seriously, you know what I mean. Why did you come back?"

"Does there have to be a reason?" Adam tilted his head, those eyes still drilling into her. "Can't a guy just want to come back to his roots?"

"Sure." Faye hesitated. Her gut instincts weren't usually wrong, but then no one had affected her like Adam had as of late. "But usually, a guy like you who left to find something different wouldn't come back unless it was for a good reason."

"And joining my family business isn't a good reason?"

She flushed. That's not what she was getting at. She didn't even know what she was getting at. Faye shook her head and slouched back into her seat. "Never mind. Forget I said anything." First the conversation about him carrying her in the rain, and now this. Why was it that she couldn't catch a break? The second she started seeing Adam in a different way, everything just felt uncomfortable.

The sound of their discomfort was the loudest thing in that whole diner. She was just about to shoot out of her seat and demand that he take her back home so she could be embarrassed in private, but then he broke the silence.

"Actually, you're right."

Faye lifted her face and stared at him in disbelief.

He chuckled and then scratched his cheek before looking away. "My dad was getting to a point in his life where he was looking at retirement. He was working fewer hours, and Bridget was taking on more than she should have. I heard about it, and I told him I'd come home to take over. I'm sure Bridget wasn't all that thrilled about that, though."

"Why not? Doesn't she care about your father?"

"Oh, she does. I think she sees him as more of a father than either of us realize—more than I've been a son to him. I probably should have let him just leave the shop to Bridget and stay put like you said."

"I never said…"

"No, but you inferred it. I could have stayed in the city and started my own thing. Bridget was handling things here. I guess I might have been triggered in a way. I didn't want to see the shop go to someone who wasn't in the family." Adam offered her a chagrined smile. "Go ahead. Tell me I'm shallow and that I shouldn't have come just for that reason."

Faye leaned forward. "I would never tell you that."

"Oh? Why's that?"

"Because you still came back for your dad."

Adam snorted. "I came back so I could take over."

"To let your father retire."

The look on his face made it clear he had no idea what she was trying to get at.

Faye fidgeted in her seat. "Think about it. Your father could have retired any time he wanted as soon as Bridget started working for him. Now he's getting serious about it. He's working even fewer hours, letting you take over more. He's finally getting serious about retirement. I don't think he would have done that if you weren't here to facilitate that. Sure, you came here thinking it was for you, but in reality, it was for him."

His tight expression softened. "I never thought of it that way." Adam shook his head and let out a strained chuckle. "But that doesn't change one fact."

Faye tilted her head. "What is that?"

"I came here with one thing in mind. You can't say a guy is a good person if something admirable also occurred at the same time as their less-than-worthy decision. What if a robber broke into someone's house to find someone they presumed dead on the kitchen floor so it scared them away. But the person wasn't dead, and the broken window was the only thing to clear out the carbon dioxide gas that had knocked the person out. Is that robber a good person?"

She scoffed at him. "Are you seriously trying to give me an ethics lesson?"

He sobered. "No."

"Yes, you are." She laughed. "You're trying to convince me you're not a good person when you are. It's not gonna work, you know. Because you're not a robber. And after you got here, you didn't leave. You're still helping your father. And you're still helping me."

This time Adam didn't have anything to say. For whatever reason, she had thrown him off guard.

Faye gave him a smug smile. "See? You can't argue with that. You had your out, but you came back."

He was silent long enough that she started to wonder if she'd said something that frustrated him. That would be ridiculous. Didn't he want to be a good person? Maybe he didn't. There were a certain number of guys out there who actually liked to be viewed as "bad."

No, not bad.

Dangerous.

Faye snickered.

Adam stiffened. "What?"

"What?"

"You laughed. What are you laughing at? Do you find my decisions funny?"

"No! I was thinking of something else."

He frowned.

Faye let out a groan. "You're not going to make this a big

thing, are you? Aren't you tired of all of these strained conversations?"

"Strained conversations?"

She dragged her hand down her face. It was already getting hot. "How about we get going?"

"Not until you tell me what you were laughing about."

If she could drop her face on the table and avoid this conversation, she would. "It was just a silly thought."

A smile stretched across Adam's face. "Then you can tell me what it was about."

"It's really none of your business." She got up from her place at the table. "And if you don't want to drive me home because I won't tell you, then don't. I'll just find another way home."

He stood. "Over my dead body."

She blinked. That wasn't the reaction she'd expected from him. "Okay. Then let's go." Faye reached for her purse and got to her feet. "I guess I'll be seeing you on Saturday next week then—at the shop?"

"I'm free tomorrow." He shrugged on his jacket and strode away without saying another word.

She remained frozen to her spot, her eyes following him. They hadn't done anything on Sundays before now. It had always been Saturdays. Why was he changing this on her?

Her mouth dropped open and she charged after him, catching up right as they made it outside. The rain had stopped and they were left with the remnants of a hefty storm. All around them on the pavement were puddles that wouldn't soon evaporate. The buildings dripped with the rain that still clung to the surfaces and humidity hung in the air. Faye hurried toward him and tapped him on the shoulder a little harder than she'd expected, causing him to flinch.

Adam turned around and stared at her. "What was that for?"

"Just because I didn't want to have a certain conversation with you doesn't mean you can just boss me around. I get that you want to spend the least amount of time with me that you can, but you don't have to be so obvious about it."

"Excuse me?"

"Scheduling our mechanic stuff tomorrow instead of next week as planned. You're trying to get this done and over with early, aren't you?" She had her hands on her hips, and at this point, she was probably making a bigger scene than was necessary. A few people had given them strange looks, but she cared more about what he was suggesting with this change of schedule.

If she was honest with herself, she'd probably admit that this had more to do with wanting to spend as much time with him as she could and she was hurt he didn't feel the same.

Adam's gaze darted back and forth among the patrons who wandered around them. He worked his jaw before suddenly grasping her upper arm and tugging her to the side out of the path of anyone who might overhear their conversation.

"What are you talking about?" he hissed. "That's not what this is about at all."

12

Adam

 dam pulled Faye into the shadow of the building, his heart pounding more erratically than it should. He stared down into Faye's unassuming gaze, hating the way understanding not only washed over him but also how it must be making her feel.

How could she assume he didn't want to spend time with her? Hadn't he just said he was available to meet tomorrow? Racking his brain, he couldn't find where he'd given her any indication that would support her accusation.

"What are you talking about?" he repeated.

Faye looked down where his hand grasped her arm. His attention dipped there then he released her as if she were a hot iron. She scowled at him, folding her arms. "If you don't want to continue our arrangement, you can tell me. You don't have to speed it up so—"

He shook his head and let out a heavy sigh. "That's the most ridiculous thing you've said all day."

Her mouth dropped open, but at least she wasn't spewing those absurd words.

Adam ducked his face lower, closer to hers. "When I said I wanted to see you tomorrow, it wasn't to speed up our arrangement." He let his statement settle in. His jaw ached from the amount of pressure he put on it. She didn't verbally ask him to clarify, but her eyes did. Faye didn't move even though he was close enough that he could smell her perfume. At any moment she could have stepped back. She could have pushed him away. But she didn't.

He didn't know if that fact was the thing that drove him forward or if it was something else entirely. "I offered to work on your mom's truck tomorrow because I want to see you again."

A bark of laughter burst from Faye's lips, causing him to jump back. "You're kidding."

"I assure you, I'm dead serious."

"Like I said, you can tell me the truth. I can handle it."

Adam arched a single brow, moving closer to her again. "Your reaction when you thought I didn't want to spend time with you proves otherwise." This time he folded his arms and tilted his head. "How about you explain *that*. Why is it that you would be unhappy if we were to cut our arrangement short?"

She snapped her mouth shut, sobering. This time she did back away. In a swift movement, she turned away from him and strode down the sidewalk. She wove between groups of people, her hands forming little balls.

For a second he was caught off guard. Was she actually storming away from him? Adam lurched forward, following in her wake. "Faye!" he called after her. "Faye, where are you going?" When he caught up to her, he didn't bother touching her or forcing her to stop. Something about the way she was holding herself was different.

Her guard was up. She didn't want to talk. Well, that was how most of the evening had gone. Adam couldn't recall the last time he'd had such a strange encounter with a woman. "You know, when a guy takes a girl on a date, he doesn't expect it to go quite like this."

Faye stopped suddenly and faced him. "This wasn't a date."

"It wasn't? Because I brought you here. I paid for your food, and I—"

She poked him in the chest a little harder than was necessary.

He grunted and rubbed the sore spot with his fingers.

"You have a girlfriend."

"What? No, I don't."

"Well, you have a girl you like."

His mouth opened then he shut it just as quickly. At the rate of this crazy conversation, he wasn't so sure he wanted to see just how much further she might take this. Faye was different. And he wasn't entirely turned off by her. Adam cleared his throat and nodded. "Sure. I like Dahlia."

"Exactly. You like her so much you were willing to do free labor on my truck that had a ton of work that needed to be done."

"You're right again."

"So this isn't a date."

"Faye," he sighed, "just because I ask you on a date doesn't mean it has to be romantic."

And just like that, the little puffer fish with all the spines deflated. Faye's shoulders dropped and she let out a soft breath.

He forced a chuckle because, up until this very moment, he'd been far too tempted to tell her he might just like more than one person, and he wanted to get to know her just as much as he wanted to get to know Dahlia. But that didn't sound like such a good idea in his head anymore.

Adam cleared his throat and let out a strangled cough. "I like you, Faye. You're funny, smart, and easy to be around... well, except for today. I thought maybe it might be fun to do another day's worth of work this weekend with my friend."

Inwardly he cringed. That word was the nail in the coffin for anything he might have wanted to pursue with Faye. She'd hear that word, and she'd never look at him the same way. It was just as well because the second they'd started talking about serious matters, she'd turned into something different. He'd scared her off.

A myriad of emotions crossed her face. Surprise, relief, and embarrassment were only a few of the ones he recognized. He was just grateful she'd relaxed.

There was just one problem.

He couldn't do the same thing.

For a reason he could only assume was his continued growing interest in her, his whole body had woken up like never before. Yes, his heart was getting a workout, but more than that, every nerve ending, every synapse in his brain, was telling him he needed to fix this. How could he be so careless as to put himself into the friend zone?

Such a rookie mistake!

Adam gestured the way they'd come. "If you want to go home, I'll take you there, but if you still have some time this evening, we could do something else. Maybe something with less awkward conversations?"

She laughed.

Thank goodness for humor because he was drowning right now.

"What do you have in mind?" She shoved her hands into her back pockets and didn't meet his gaze for long. It was getting later, darker, but he could see the faint flush that filled her cheeks.

"I dunno. I guess we could go for a walk? I didn't really plan on it turning out like this tonight."

Faye laughed again.

Any rational person would ask him what he saw in her. They'd think he was nuts for even finding her attractive—not on the surface, but beneath.

Adam knew better than to judge her for their evening. She was strongly independent, for one. Faye was the kind of girl who figured out what she wanted, and she went for it. She figured out how to solve her own problems in a way that made sense. Faye was smart, too. She'd have to be in order to notice the small nuances that came with her situation with her family. When she'd discussed how she felt about finding her place, it had stuck with him.

And those were just the two biggest reasons. Of course there were a lot more. Like the way her laugh was contagious or the way she took charge on a horse. And today when she'd lifted her face to the rain—her beauty rivaled even that of Dahlia.

"You coming?"

Adam jumped. His eyes refocused on Faye only to find the space she'd occupied was empty. He turned around and found her right behind him.

"You okay?" She chuckled. "Maybe we *were meant* to be friends. I never thought I'd meet someone who could zone off like I do. Come on. Let's go find something fun to do."

He fell into step beside her. "Like what?"

She shrugged. "Well, we're in town. That rules out riding or anything on the ranch unless you want to head that way. The rodeo won't be in Copper Creek for another couple of weeks. I guess that leaves us with bowling or axe throwing."

"*Axe throwing*? You're joking, right?"

Faye laughed again and the sound alone was enough to set his blood roaring. Why did he have to chicken out at the last minute and not tell her exactly where his affection stood? Because that would have scared her off, and he knew it. Time to get past that and make the most of the time he had with her tonight. She glanced at him out of the corner of her eye. "You haven't been axe throwing yet?"

He shook his head. "I didn't even know that was a thing."

"I suppose it's fairly new. Most people like to spend their time at the country club, but it's so crowded there—and the rodeo too—I'd rather spend my time somewhere I can actually think."

"And that's throwing axes."

Her smile widened. "Hey, it's better than going to a shooting range."

"But it's throwing axes."

She stopped, her hands on her hips in that trademark way that was so purely Faye he wouldn't have her any other way. "What? Do you not believe I can do it?"

"Oh, I know you can do it. I just didn't think..." There was no good way of saying what came to his mind. Faye was more than a force to be reckoned with. He'd have to stay on guard if he wanted to continue getting closer to her.

Her head tilted to the side and her eyes danced. "What?"

Adam shook his head.

"Come on. You have to tell me now."

He shook his head again. "You didn't tell me why *you*

laughed." The moment of peace only lasted for the blink of an eye.

She let out a sigh and rolled her eyes. "I laughed because I realized something."

"Yeah? What was that?"

"You're a guy."

He bit back a smile. "Impressive. It usually takes folks around here a few months to figure that out."

She rolled her eyes again and shoved him this time. "What I *mean* is that, as a guy, you probably want to be seen as a 'bad-boy' or someone who is 'dangerous.'"

"And that's laughable because..."

"Because you're the furthest thing from dangerous that I know."

That statement wounded him a little more than he cared to admit. No, he didn't want to be considered *dangerous*—not to Faye, at least. Did he want her to view him as someone who could hold his own and protect her? Of course. But *dangerous*? That wasn't who he was.

The fact that she laughed only rubbed salt in the wound. Was it so unfathomable that he could be that kind of guy?

She sobered far too quickly and reached out with her hand. "I'm sorry. See? That's why I didn't want to tell you. I knew it would hurt your feelings. It's okay. Guys don't have to be tough all the time."

"And girls don't have to be dainty, damsels in distress," he muttered.

"Exactly! Thank you. That's my point. I can be strong but still like to be carried—" She cut herself off and looked away. "The axe-throwing thing is just up the street."

"Hold on." He pushed forward, coming up next to her as they walked side by side. "You actually liked it when I carried you to the house, didn't you?"

"Will you stop with the carrying thing? We don't have to discuss it." There was only a mild note of irritation in her voice, but it was strong enough for him to notice.

You were the one who brought it up was on the tip of his tongue. They could start another little argument. Or he could let it drop. Clearly, she didn't like to have this kind of attention on her. Faye didn't want to admit that she might actually like the attention he was giving her. It was strange making that realization—and even harder for him to stop himself from teasing her.

So instead of pointing it out, he clasped his hands behind his back and walked by her side. They passed a few stores where the display windows were already turned off. She didn't bring up when he'd refused to complete his statement about her being the kind of girl who would enjoy the axe-throwing thing. But the more he thought about it, the more he realized this was exactly the kind of thing Faye would be into.

She liked to work on her truck. She liked to be out on the horses. She liked adventure and risk. Why else would she brush off his concerns about the storm? Faye was just like a wild horse that had been trained but not broken.

And that was when he realized just why he liked her so much.

Working on cars was mechanical, literally and theoretically. Every part had a place, a purpose. When one didn't work, it was replaced. There was a certain way to do said replacement, and when it was taken care of, the rest of the car fell into line.

He was used to that sort of life—where everything made sense.

On the other end, he was raised in a town with cowboys—who were pretty much the definition of chaos.

It wasn't a bad chaos. On the contrary, it was exciting and

thrilling to see the men riding their horses at the rodeos. But they were so much more than that.

Faye was so much more.

She couldn't be tamed.

And yet she chose to stay.

One day she might realize that she could go somewhere else—be something else. Maybe she'd already figured that part out. And yet, she'd stayed. She was like a wild stallion who knew exactly how to escape and yet made a conscious decision to remain here. It was admirable and something he'd never done himself.

Adam looked at her out of the corner of his eye. Much like the mechanics of cars, the world would continue to make sense in certain ways. His infatuation with Faye fell into that realm of understanding. Adam found there was always a reason when something caught his attention. Sometimes it was because a part didn't fit right.

But other times it was like tonight when the universe told him to be patient. The reveal would come, and it was going to be amazing.

13

Faye

Faye's chin rested in her hand as she stared off at the landscape before her. She couldn't seem to wrap her head around the way things had gone over the weekend. It felt like she had been on one of those carnival rides that left her dizzy and wondering if she'd left her stomach behind.

As if reacting to her thoughts, her gut clenched and turned over. On top of that, her face flushed even though there was no one around to be embarrassed for—only herself.

How had she gotten to this point? She'd allowed herself to develop feelings for a guy who was obviously not interested in her. He had a girl he was willing to go to great lengths in order to impress.

Then that stupid little argument they had about him not wanting to spend time with her. That couldn't have been more mortifying than if she'd admitted to telling him she had a small crush on him.

She covered her face with her hands and let out a groan.

Friends.

He wanted to be *friends*.

Even though Faye hadn't been in a traditional relationship before, she knew what it meant to be put in the friend zone. She'd never get him to see her as anything else. What was worse was the fact that after they had that conversation, he had changed the way he acted around her. He kept his distance from her, and it was almost like his body was stiffer.

Faye shouldn't have said anything. She should have just let things be and seen how things played out. Adam would be crazy to want anything to do with her now, so she might as well force herself to move on.

"Everything okay? Are there problems with the truck?"

Faye's head popped up to find Grace and Eloise coming up the porch steps. They were clad in boots and their riding gear, a blush of a brisk morning ride present on their faces.

Grace sat in the chair on the other side of the small table where Faye had placed her mug, and Eloise opted to lean against the railing of the porch.

Faye shook her head. "Nothing is wrong with the truck. Everything is going according to schedule," she muttered bitterly.

Grace chuckled as she glanced in Eloise's direction. "Sounds like it." Sarcasm dripped from her voice. "I told you it wasn't worth fixing the truck, but you just had to—"

"This isn't about the truck."

Grace snapped her mouth shut and lifted her brows. "Okay. Well, something is clearly bothering you."

"Well, maybe it's none of your business."

Her younger sister lifted her hands, the look on her face saying it all as she got to her feet and went inside.

Eloise shook her head, laughing under her breath. "That wasn't very nice, Faye."

"I don't care," she muttered.

Her older sister moved across the porch and took the seat Grace had vacated. "I think you might want to reconsider how you're treating Grace, considering how she was willing to give you mom's truck in the first place. And isn't Riley footing the bill for the parts?"

"Yeah," Faye groaned. "You're right. I blew it."

She laughed again. "I'm sure she'll be fine. You can apologize later. So what's the matter if it's not the truck?"

Faye's eyes cut to Eloise before she shook her head. "You wouldn't understand."

"I could try."

Eloise had been dating more lately. She hadn't found anyone to be serious with, but she was out in the world experiencing what none of them had before finding their soulmates. All of Faye's sisters besides Brielle were now in serious relationships, and Brielle wasn't in one due to personal preferences.

"Why aren't you dating?"

"I *am* dating." Eloise tilted her head.

"No, I mean, why haven't you found anyone to be serious with?"

Her eyes widened, but before she could say anything, Faye cut her off.

"I'm not dating anyone either. I'm just curious how come you've been going on so many dates but haven't found one you want to be serious with?"

Eloise's eyes narrowed and her lips quirked into a sly smile.

Faye sighed. "I promise there's a reason I'm asking this, but it's not for the reason you think. Just answer the question."

Her sister leaned back into the wooden porch chair and shifted her focus to the landscape that surrounded their home. "I suppose it's because I don't want to settle down with the first guy who asks me out. I want to make sure I know what I want before I let that happen."

"You don't think that everyone else did the same?"

Eloise laughed. "I *know* they didn't." She faced Faye and her expression turned serious. "Each of our sisters was thrown into a relationship without even considering the consequences of discovering they might be incompatible. There is no such thing as love at first sight. Just ask Brielle. She knows. There are as many different guys with different personalities out there as there are different breeds of horses. And not all of them are going to be the kind of guy you want to end up with. Why settle for something when you haven't seen it all?"

Faye hated how much sense her sister was making. She'd allowed herself to get so caught up in her developing feelings for Adam that she hadn't allowed herself to take a look around to see if there was anyone else who might be a better fit. It wasn't very smart on her part.

Juvenile, in fact.

"So what does this have to do with your sour mood? Did you ask someone out and they turned you down?"

Her head whipped around and she stared at Eloise. "No. There's no one I'm interested in that way." It was a lie, and she knew better than to try to pull it off. All the Callahan girls knew how to read the others. It was a blessing and a curse they were gifted with by not being allowed any outside relationships.

It just turned out that Eloise was willing to overlook the fib at this moment.

Faye cleared her throat and dragged her focus away from her sister so she could try to cover up any other lies that might tumble out. "I was just thinking that I needed to get out there. We're not getting any younger, and I have to dive in at some point, right?"

"That's what I think," Eloise offered.

"So how did you get started? Do you go to town and just pick up guys? Or what?"

Her sister laughed. Why did it feel like she was laughing at Faye and not just at the situation itself? Faye scowled, crossing her arms. She didn't even really want to go on any dates with someone else. She just knew if she didn't, she'd end up feeling like she was some poor unfortunate country girl watching the guy she liked go after someone who didn't deserve him.

Eloise reached over the small table and placed her hand on Faye's arm. "If you want to go on some dates, you just have to ask. I'm sure I could get a few set up for you. We could go on a couple doubles. But if you don't want to do that, you could just come with us to the country club on the weekends and go dancing with the guys who aren't there with dates. Well, one time a guy asked me to dance and I *know* he was there with a date."

Faye wrinkled her nose. "That doesn't sound all that great. How did his date feel?"

Eloise shrugged. "I have no idea. He ended up asking me out a few weeks later."

Lifting her brows, Faye shook her head. "Men are disgusting."

Her sister snickered. "Yeah, well, they can't all smell like roses. It wasn't like he had a girlfriend, and he didn't ask me out when he was on his date."

"Maybe I don't want to go on any dates after all. This all sounds like politics but worse."

"You're not wrong." Eloise poked Faye's upper arm. "Hey, what about that guy you've been taking riding? You could ask him out."

And just like that, Faye's face flushed red-hot. "*No.*"

Eloise blinked. "Why not? Is he really that bad?"

"No, he's just not interested in me. He's got a girl he's trying to impress. I doubt that asking him out would do me any good." On the contrary, it would probably destroy her heart. The whole point of getting out into the dating world was so Faye had something to take her mind off Adam. It didn't hurt that she might be able to compare him to others as well and hopefully realize he wasn't the guy for her. "On second thought, sure, why not?"

"Why not, what?"

"Set me up. Or let's go dancing. Whatever you want to do, I'll do it." She grimaced. "Except I can't do it on Saturday. It will have to be Friday night because I'm still working with Adam on Saturdays." She might be working on Sundays, too. There was no telling what the new schedule might be.

Eloise's expression lit up like a Christmas tree. "That's great. I just know you're going to have so much fun. Brielle has been a little bit of a drag lately. She refuses to go to the club right now because of you know who…"

Faye frowned. "Because of who?"

"You know. Shane. The guy who owns the place. They went on a few dates, and she doesn't want to see him anymore."

"But she's not seeing him."

Eloise shook her head and her voice lowered almost conspiratorially. "No. I mean, she literally doesn't want to see him. I'm telling you, that was probably the first breakup that happened like that. You know she'd been dating before dad gave us the green light, right?"

Faye nodded.

"Well, from what I understand, they typically ended on good terms. But not this one. I don't know why." Eloise shrugged and her expression returned to one full of excitement. "This is going to be so much fun. I just know you're going to love it.

THE NOISE in the country club was a lot louder than Faye had expected. The people moved like wheat in the fields as it swayed in the wind. It made her nauseous. This was why she preferred to be out on her saddle in the middle of nowhere.

Even the axe throwing was better than this.

Eloise was at the bar, leaning against the counter and chatting up the male bartender. They'd opted to go stag tonight, meaning they didn't have dates. And now Faye was really regretting it. At least if she had an official date, she'd have someone to talk to. As it was, she was a literal wallflower off by herself.

If she'd been the one to drive, she would have left by now. Eloise was in her element and Faye didn't want to mess up a good thing.

Faye lifted her drink to her lips and took a sip. The cola burned her throat going down, reminding her why she preferred non-carbonated beverages. She should have just gotten water with a lemon.

A sigh rumbled through her chest as a new song started. She might just give her father a call to see if he could pick her up from this nightmare. At least then she wouldn't be stepping on anyone's toes. This was a mistake.

"Faye? I didn't know you came here."

Every fiber of Faye's being froze. Even with the hum of

voices and the loud music, she recognized that voice. She prayed she was wrong. Adam was a busy guy. He didn't have time to come to the country club on a Friday night. Slowly she turned to face the voice.

She was wrong.

Adam smiled at her, and her insides melted. Great. That was why she wanted to be here with someone else. She needed someone to take her mind off the way he affected her. He moved closer to her, and it took every ounce of willpower to not step back.

"How are you doing?" he asked.

"Good. What are you doing here?"

His smile deepened and he gestured around them. "This is sorta the best place to be on a Friday night, right?"

"Right." Her face burned. Just her luck. Why did he have to be here? Then her frustration shifted into something else—something with a tad bit of hope. Maybe he could be her date—purely in a friend sort of way. She ran her hand through her hair and offered a small smile. "Actually, it's great that you're—"

"Here's your drink, Adam." A tall, skinny girl in heels and a skirt that was a little too short joined their small group. Her dark hair hung around her shoulders in waves, and she wore makeup that was way too thick. Her eyes trailed up and down Faye's body, and Faye could have sworn the woman sneered at her. "Who's this?"

Faye bristled. When she'd first seen Dahlia, she'd thought she was pretty enough. But there was something about hearing her speak that sounded like nails on a chalkboard.

Adam gestured toward Faye with his glass. "This is Faye Callahan. I'm helping her work on her mother's truck."

All at once the woman's expression changed. It was like a button had been pushed. She was no longer threatened by

Faye whatsoever. "Oh. Isn't Adam the best? He helped fix my brother's truck a couple months back."

Faye swallowed back the words she'd planned on saying. Adam had finally done it. He'd grown the courage necessary to ask her out, and by the looks of it, he was very successful. Faye forced a smile.

"He is *just* the best." She needed an escape. There was no way she could stick around now. Not when she didn't have anyone to help her keep her mind off what had transpired.

A cowboy wandered past and without thinking, Faye reached out and grabbed his arm. "There you are honey. I wasn't sure where you went off to."

To his credit, the cowboy stranger didn't immediately pull his arm from her grasp. He glanced from her to her company. An easy smile crossed his face, and he touched the brim of his hat. "I was just coming to look for you, too."

"You ready to get going? I'm not feeling too well." She hoped his first reaction wasn't just a fluke. All he had to do was agree and escort her outside. She'd figure it out from there.

Sure enough, the guy came to her rescue. He nodded. "Of course. Let's get you home so you can get some rest."

Faye could feel Adam's eyes on her, but she didn't dare look at him. Maybe she could text him or call him and let him know she wouldn't be teaching him tomorrow. After seeing him with his dream girl, she didn't think she'd be up for the couple of hours she'd have to supervise him in the corral. She offered the couple a weak smile, not meeting Adam's eyes. "It was nice to see you."

Mystery man walked her toward the door, letting her keep her hand in the crook of his arm until they made it out onto the front steps. A blast of cold air cooled her cheeks and took the edge off her roiling stomach.

Faye immediately dropped her hand and leaned against a railing that blocked them from going off the edge. "I'm so sorry," she blustered, "I shouldn't have pulled you into that."

He snapped his fingers and pointed one at her. "You're not a Callahan, are you?"

Her eyes darted up to meet his. "I am."

"Now this makes sense. Which one are you?"

Faye frowned. "I'm sorry. Who are you?"

"Wade. Wade Keagan. I've worked with Brielle a little bit out at my ranch." He glanced toward the door. "Is she here tonight by chance?"

She shook her head. "No, I'm sorry." The silence grew between them until she lurched into motion. "Anyway, thanks for your help. But I'll let you get back in there. You probably have a date—"

"Nah. No date." He crossed his arms, studying her as he tilted his head. "You need a ride? I'm headed that way."

Faye fidgeted, her eyes drifting toward the door. Wade seemed to be the answer to her problems, and if Brielle knew him, maybe accepting his help wouldn't be so bad. She could just message Eloise and tell her she got a ride home. "Yeah, okay. That would be a big help. Thank you."

"Don't mention it."

14

Adam

Adam picked up his phone, but only five minutes had passed. Faye remembered that they had their riding lesson this week. She had to. He'd expected to hear from her last night or early this morning after she left the country club not feeling well.

But there had been radio silence.

In hindsight, he probably shouldn't have just shown up on the Callahan ranch without getting at least something from her. Now he was standing in her barn waiting for her arrival. He didn't dare go up to her house and knock on the door, though he didn't know why.

Bella stood in her stall, bobbing her head as if she knew exactly what they should be doing. He had half a mind to try to put the saddle on her and just take her out to the corral. He didn't know what Faye might do if she saw him through her window.

But something stopped him. The last thing he needed was to have Mr. Callahan marching across the property and asking him what he thought he was doing.

Maybe Adam should just head home and cut his losses. Clearly, Faye was seeing someone. Maybe that guy wasn't thrilled about their arrangement. Then again, she might actually not feel well. Wasn't that what she'd said when she left the country club last night?

The more he contemplated this, the closer he came to the realization that he really shouldn't have come at all. There was being presumptuous and then there was crossing a line, and he'd done the latter.

Adam rubbed Bella's nose one final time and turned to head out of the barn when he had to stop in his tracks. In the doorway stood a silhouette. It was definitely female, but he wasn't sure if Faye had come to find him or if this was one of her sisters.

He squinted at the figure, hesitating. Did all her sisters know about this arrangement? Would they let him ride without a supervisor? He'd been getting closer to his riding goals, and he didn't want to stop now.

The woman still didn't move. There was no way he was imagining this. She was definitely there. So what was she expecting?

His stomach churned. A stranger in her barn was probably not what she'd expected to find on a Saturday morning. He was lucky she didn't pull a shotgun off the wall and shoot him with it. Adam cleared his throat and took a step toward her. The worst that could happen was that she would run screaming to the house and attract all kinds of unwanted attention. As soon as he got close enough to confirm this was not indeed Faye, he waved his hand and called out to her.

"I'm here to see Faye. Is she around?"

The woman placed her hands on her hips and then leaned backward far enough that he could only imagine her looking toward the house. She muttered something under her breath and shook her head. "Yeah. She's here. I'll go get her for you."

"Thanks... um..."

"It's Bri." She strode away, and he could have sworn he heard her mutter something about Faye deserving what was coming to her.

Adam hovered in the doorway to the barn. Now that Faye was being fetched, he didn't feel like he needed to leave necessarily, but he wasn't sure how she'd respond to him coming when they didn't clear a meeting.

What was he thinking? He wasn't usually this on edge. They had an arrangement. He shouldn't feel awkward for coming when this was the plan all along. He just needed to stop reading too much into what had happened yesterday.

As his thoughts drifted in that direction, Adam couldn't help but compare his evening with Dahlia to his evening with Faye the week before. They were so vastly different from one another, except for one major similarity. They were both headstrong women who knew what they wanted and how to get it when it came down to it.

He just hadn't expected to find that Dahlia wanted *him*. Bumping into her as he had arrived at the country club had been a strange coincidence but not as odd as bumping into Faye. After she'd left, he'd spent the majority of the evening with Dahlia. It wasn't an entirely unpleasant way to spend his Friday night. Except he couldn't seem to stop his thoughts from shifting to Faye. He was distracted, and it wasn't just because she left with that cowboy.

Or maybe it was.

"I'm so sorry."

He jumped, forcing himself to focus on Faye. She was

actively pulling her hair into a ponytail. It almost looked like she had just woken up. But that couldn't be right. Cowboys were supposed to get up with the sun—or earlier.

"You okay?"

Her eyes darted to meet his before she looked down and crouched to adjust her pant leg in her boot. "Yeah. Why?"

"You just... I've never known you to be late."

Once more she glanced at him but only briefly. "Yeah, well, I had a late night."

"With that guy?"

Her hands stilled. Actually, her whole body seemed to freeze. His assumptions were correct. She was with that guy for who knows how late? A sharp pain ripped through his chest, settling with a thud in his stomach. It felt like he'd been hit by a heavy rock that had somehow caught on fire before it made contact. She got to her feet and nodded toward the barn.

"We should get started so we can head out to the pastures. I'm going to see if I can teach you how to rope a calf."

Adam's jaw tightened. Why wasn't she answering the question? He turned on his heel, following her into the barn. The question still burned in his mind, but he knew he couldn't ask again. He couldn't even inquire about the guy's name without sounding jealous. "It was weird seeing you at the club last night."

No answer.

"I don't think I've ever seen you there before. Was that your first time?"

She shot him a disgruntled look. "Are you inferring that I don't get out much?"

"Do you?"

Faye snorted. "That is no business of yours."

"Really? That's how you're going to play this?"

"I'm not playing anything. I just don't want to talk about personal stuff."

As if guided by a force that was not his own, he reached out and grasped her upper arm. "Wait a doggone minute. I thought we'd decided it was okay for us to be friends. You're helping me, and I'm helping you."

Her expression softened. "You're right."

Adam dropped his hand. "Heck yeah, I'm right. Let's have a conversation that doesn't feel like I'm trying to pull your teeth."

That statement got a smile. The weight in his stomach eased, if only a little bit.

"Fine. How about you tell me how you managed to get the beautiful Dahlia to go on a date with you last night. I thought you said she wasn't interested in you unless you could ride in the rodeo." Her voice held a slight teasing note to it, but it was laced with something else he couldn't place.

As much as he wanted to investigate it, he knew better. Adam grabbed the saddle and placed it on Bella's back. This work had become second nature, almost like changing a tire or refilling the fluids under the hood of his truck. "I didn't think she *was* interested in me. It just sort of happened." He should be thrilled. But all he could think about was Faye and her date—how it had ended and why she was up so late. "Your turn."

She shook her head right before she ducked to cinch the belt beneath Blaze's belly. "Not so fast. I want to know how your date went. Did you take her home? Was there a kiss involved?"

Again, that strange teasing tone was mingled with something else. It sounded foreign and hard on his ears. He shot her a look before resuming his work. "What is there to tell?

We danced. We talked. No, we didn't kiss. I like to know the girl a little better before I do something like that."

"So, I guess there's another date lined up."

Adam shrugged. "Yeah, I guess. Though I'd really like to learn a little more about these horses before I do that. It's hard talking about what I'm learning when I barely know what I'm doing." He gave her a wry smile. "The problem with wanting to impress a cowgirl with knowledge about horses is that she already knows what there is to know. I can't exactly win."

Faye snorted. "Dahlia isn't a cowgirl. She's a rodeo groupie. I doubt she knows as much as you do at this point."

He stilled, his hands fingering the lead rope he'd just put on Bella. Now he knew exactly what that tone was. Faye was jealous. It couldn't have been clearer. Only jealousy didn't make much sense at the moment because she had found someone to date, too. "Actually, she's a barrel racer."

She snorted. "Same difference."

Adam turned to study her while she finished saddling Blaze. There was no indication she had found a new romantic interest. Women were funny that way. He'd seen it time and time again when they came into the shop. They might have conversations on their phones with their friends, or he might overhear them talking to someone who came with them for the repair.

There was one thing all women possessed when they found someone they were excited to date. It was this... for lack of a better word... *glow* about them. It was as if this new love was enough to fuel their soul—feed it and help them float from one thing to another.

Guys? Well, they were different. They were happier. They might even be more willing to hear bad news. But they didn't talk as much in public places about the girl they were seeing. They were just generally in a good mood.

Faye's eyes caught his, but for once he didn't care if she knew he was staring. He moved to the stall wall and crossed his arms over the top of it. "Okay. Your turn. Who was the cowboy who took you home last night."

"That's none of your business."

Adam laughed. "That's not fair. I told you my story. It's your turn to tell me yours. I'd wager you already talked about it with one or more of your sisters. Should I go track down Brielle and ask her who he was?"

Faye's eyes widened and the blood drained from her face before erupting like a volcano and flooding her cheeks with scarlet. "Don't you dare."

He chuckled again. "So she does know what happened. I'm really curious now because she didn't seem to be all that thrilled this morning."

She shook her head as she broke eye contact. "It doesn't matter because I won't be seeing him anymore." Her hand rammed against the stall door as she pushed it open and headed down the aisle without him. Wow. She was in a bad mood—worse than her sister was.

Instantly he felt a little guilty over bringing up the cowboy at all. Had something happened between the three of them that he wasn't aware of? That painful twisted feeling returned to his stomach. There were a number of reasons why two sisters would be upset regarding a man, but the one that came to mind first was that they might be fighting over him.

Except Faye just said she wasn't going to see him again.

He jogged to catch up to Faye and did so just as they exited the building. "Did something happen with your cowboy?"

"He's *not* my cowboy," she muttered bitterly.

"Not anymore?"

She stopped and whirled around to face him, her eyes flashing. "What is your problem? You're nosier than all those women in town who don't have anything better to do than gossip about who is seeing who in this community. If you want to cluck like a hen, then there's the hen house." She jabbed a finger to her left, all the while retaining eye contact. "I don't have time to gossip about who I'm seeing or not seeing. I don't mind being your friend, but that doesn't mean all conversation is on the table. Now do you want to ride today or not?"

Adam pressed his lips together firmly. Their relationship, or what it had been, had changed over the course of a week, and he had no idea why. And maybe that was the reason why he snapped. "You're what's wrong with people these days."

"What?" she scoffed.

"You don't know how to talk to people—to connect with people. Sometimes people ask questions because they care. Have you ever considered that? Last I checked, we're friends. And as such, I should be able to talk to you when something is bothering you and not get my head bitten off."

"You want to know what's bothering me?"

"I wouldn't have asked if I didn't." Though their voices remained at a typical level, the tones with which they were speaking had turned hard. If they were friends before, they weren't friends anymore.

Then again, maybe he'd never truly been her friend.

Because he wanted something more.

She poked him hard in the chest.

"*Ow.*"

"You. You're what's bothering me."

"Me? Are you kidding me? What did I do?"

She threw her hands into the air. "Everything. Nothing. You're just you."

He couldn't help it. He let out a laugh. "Oh, I knew you were a little crazy, but I didn't think it would go this far."

"You think I'm crazy? What kind of guy would think it's

smart to start learning one of the most dangerous sports there is just to impress a girl? Huh? On top of that, you're so desperate to impress her that you're willing to give away your time and expertise. It's not a fair trade-off, and you know it. I have zero idea why you would continue with this charade after you won her over. The only thing I can think of is that you don't want to burn any bridges in case you want to bring her out here for a date. Well, do it. Bring her here, take that picnic, and then you don't have to worry about coming back again."

The air in his balloon deflated and he came full circle to one single thought. She sure sounded jealous. Well, she wasn't alone.

15

———————

Faye

Faye had just lectured Adam, and yet he remained standing in front of her without moving. She wasn't expecting that. She'd practically told him to get out of there, but he wasn't budging. He was like a stray. Just waiting for her to offer him something he really wanted.

Only she couldn't figure out what that could be. What did he expect her to give him? He'd learned most of what he could when it came to riding. She was no expert on the rodeo stuff. This arrangement truly was one-sided because her truck still had several weekends to go.

Her mouth fell open and she blushed furiously.

Curse her Callahan bloodline. She'd gone and shoved her foot so far into her mouth that she was choking on it. She needed to apologize before he got wise to her and told her he was done providing free labor on her mother's truck.

Before she could do such a thing, he moved closer to her.

His sudden calm demeanor only made her antsy, but she was too terrified to move away from him.

"Are you done? Did you get it out of your system?"

She blinked. Once, twice. Then a flutter of blinking as she looked away. "I'm—oh, my gosh, I'm so sorry. I don't know what came over me. I—" She covered her face with her hand and let out a strangled laugh. "I'm so sorry."

"You said that already. Now, do you want to tell me what is really going on? I'm guessing it has something to do with that cowboy and your evening."

Her gaze darted up to meet his. Was it possible this could be so easy? Telling him she was dealing with a broken heart wasn't much of an excuse, but it was the closest thing to the truth she could tell him. She wasn't upset about Wade, though Brielle had lectured her endlessly after he asked to speak to her when he drove her home.

No, her broken heart had everything to do with the long-legged woman she saw draped all over Adam at the club.

It was entirely irrational. And she knew better than to let it bother her this much. Only her heart wasn't listening.

Faye sensed his gaze still on her and she nodded. "Yeah. It's about a cowboy."

Adam's brows lowered and his crooked grin disappeared. "He didn't hurt you, did he? Was this why Brielle was upset? Of course you don't have to tell me, but you can if it would help."

Faye let out a sigh. "Turns out he's not interested in me."

Understanding filled Adam's face. She wasn't sure, but he almost looked more relaxed, too. "Well, he's missing out," he said. "Anyone can clearly see you're worth fighting for."

She huffed. "Apparently not *everyone*."

He reached out and grasped her hand. His touch was warm, comforting, and goodness if she didn't think it was even better than she wanted it to feel. As much as she needed to pull away in that moment and not let her heart run away with this feeling, she couldn't. She stared at the way his fingers wrapped around her hand, and her thoughts took a nose-dive. He probably held Dahlia's hand, too.

That idea was all it took for reality to set in, and she tugged her hand from his to shove it in her pocket. She forced a smile she didn't feel like giving. "Thanks for listening to my crazy ramblings. I really shouldn't have taken any of this out on you."

"I don't mind." His soft voice was far too difficult to ignore, and she had to force herself to drag her eyes from where she had them locked onto his own.

She pursed her lips to the side and scooted a step back, hoping he wouldn't notice just how uncomfortable he made her feel. "How about we stick with today's plan of lassoing. If you can get the hang of that, then you can practice roping something while moving. There are a lot of events that require that kind of coordination, and they're less dangerous than bronc riding or bull riding." She turned on her heel and resumed the path she'd started when they left the barn without waiting for him to respond to her.

If a fresh start existed, she needed it in that moment. Otherwise, she'd never get over the embarrassment she felt over her tantrum. If any of her sisters had heard even a few seconds of her tirade, she'd never hear the end of it. Thankfully Brielle was still so irritated with her over having to see Wade that she opted not to be outside during this session.

Faye's eyes swept over the property in search of anyone else who might have seen or heard any of it, and her heart sank. Right there on the porch with a glass in her hand was Eloise.

Not only had she left without saying goodbye, but she'd left with a guy. A stranger.

Faye was batting a thousand this morning. Three people she'd managed to anger. When was she going to learn to just keep her big mouth shut? That's what got her in the most trouble, after all. Her big mouth.

"THAT'S IT! You're swinging it right this time." Faye sat in her saddle, watching Adam with a little more than pride. He had managed to get the post with his rope on the fifth try—something she'd never seen done from a newbie.

He had a natural talent. If he hadn't decided to work on trucks and cars, he could have very well been a cowboy.

Adam's gaze found hers as he grinned, looking more like a child than a grown man. "You see that one?"

She nodded. The air had shifted between them, though the tension wasn't completely gone. He seemed to understand where she was coming from, and he wasn't bound and determined to push her into talking about it anymore.

It was strange meeting a guy who was willing to talk about relationships with someone he wasn't dating. At least from what Faye had heard, guys just didn't do that. She couldn't decide if that was a good thing or a bad thing.

If they ended up getting closer—as friends—what would happen when he inevitably wanted to settle down with a wife? Faye couldn't imagine any woman being okay with their husband spending time with someone of the opposite sex.

That was a problem for another day.

Today she needed to focus on mending what she'd broken, though thinking about it had her stomach in knots and her face blushing so often she didn't think she had any more blood she could reroute to other parts of her body.

She itched to apologize once more, but somehow she knew it wouldn't do her any good. He'd already accepted that their conversation wasn't the norm.

Faye released a pent-up breath. "How about you get on Bella and see if you can ring that post while she's walking around it?"

"You think I could do that?"

She nodded. "You were born to do this. I can't tell you how long most guys have to work at this."

"Maybe I just have a good teacher."

She fought the blush that threatened to burst into her cheeks and barely kept it contained. "I can't take any of the credit, and you know it."

"Sure you can." He lifted one foot over the saddle and winced.

"Still feeling that burn, huh?"

"Yeah, but it's not nearly as bad as the burns you were slinging at me about thirty minutes ago."

Faye groaned. "Please tell me you're not going to hold that over my head for the rest of my life."

"For the rest of your life? Nah. Just until I get enough payback to feel like we're even."

Her laughter was unexpected. She'd managed to make a full recovery from the frustrated, jealous person she'd been when she woke up that morning. At this point, she should just be grateful that she was able to get to know him at all. Dwelling on not being able to keep his interest in a romantic sense wasn't worth her energy.

He pulled on the reins and guided Bella toward Blaze. "I've missed that today."

"Missed what?"

"Your laugh. It's nice."

Another compliment. Was it any wonder that she was developing feelings for him? He had all the qualities she'd want in a guy. Aside from the usual stuff, he also cared about his family and friends enough to stick around. He'd shown as much when he'd come home to work for his dad and refused to leave when she practically told him to less than an hour ago.

"You really shouldn't say stuff like that."

"Why not?"

Her eyes widened. Had she seriously said that out loud? Shoot! What was wrong with her? She'd asked herself this question so many times over the last few weeks that it was becoming her new mantra. Faye cleared her throat and let out a strangled laugh. Maybe he would believe she didn't know what he was talking about. "What?"

"Why shouldn't I say that your laugh is nice?"

Oh goodness. The way he said that *really* wasn't helping her move on.

"Because."

"Because why?"

She shrugged. "Because you have a girlfriend."

"Dahlia isn't my girlfriend."

Faye gave him a pointed look. "Your crush, then. It doesn't matter. Just—please treat me like you're supposed to—like a friend—so I can get back to pretending none of today actually happened."

He studied her with those clear eyes that could see into the future if he really wanted them to. She squirmed under his scrutiny, hating and loving every second his focus was on her. Finally, she couldn't take it any longer and she tore her eyes away from his. "Do a few more tries and then we need to head back. I should probably go make peace with Brielle. She wasn't too thrilled about Wade showing up on our doorstep last night."

"Why is that, exactly?"

She groaned. "Not that again. Can we just not talk about Wade anymore? I really just want to stay as far away from those conversations as I can, if possible." Faye ran her fingers through Blaze's mane, letting the coarse hair wrap around her fingers tight enough to turn her fingertips purple before she released it. She could have sworn she felt his focus on her, but when she glanced up, he had wandered farther away and was about to release the rope onto the post.

At the last second, he looked at her. His lasso missed by a few inches, and she bit back a smile. Dahlia was a lucky girl. Eloise had made some good points, but there was something she was wrong about. When a guy consumes one's thoughts to the extent that Adam consumed Faye's, there was no denying she'd found the one she wanted to be with.

Somehow Faye knew that if she dated ten, twenty, even fifty men, she'd not feel the same way about them as she did for Adam.

Was it love? Of course not.

Did she want to test the waters with anyone else?

Not on her life.

Yep, she was ruined. There was no going back from where she was, and if that meant she'd have to live her life as an old maid, so be it. She'd do what she had to in order to keep her heart intact.

They unsaddled the horses in silence. As frustrating as it was, the tension had returned the second they entered the barn. But that was probably all her fault. She'd allowed herself to watch him with the eyes of someone who desired him. Had she been smart, she wouldn't have let that happen.

Adam had shown no indication he wanted her in that way, and she needed to be okay with that.

"Hey," his quiet voice pulled her from her thoughts. She jumped, finding him standing in the stall doorway. Her eyes darted to Bella's stall and back to Adam.

"Yeah?"

"Can I ask you something?"

Faye rolled her eyes but only in an attempt to keep her heart from beating a hole out of her chest. "Not this again."

"No. Not that."

She didn't dare look at him. "What is it then?"

"I feel like you don't approve of Dahlia."

Faye snorted. "*That* is not a question."

"Why don't you like Dahlia?"

A sigh was all she could manage.

"I'm genuinely curious. What's so bad about her? Do you even know her?"

She placed a hand on her hip and faced him. "I don't have to know her to know that she's not good enough for you. Anyone that you have to change for isn't good enough for you, don't you know that?" She couldn't help the irritation from seeping into her tone.

He moved closer and she sobered. "She never asked me to change."

"But you did."

"Not really. I learned a new skill. It's like if I were to learn ballroom dancing to impress a ballerina."

"Ballerinas don't ballroom dance."

"How do you know? They could if they wanted to."

This conversation was getting ridiculous. They were already off-topic, and he had come so close to her that she had nowhere to go unless she pushed him out of the way to escape the stall.

"That's not the point. You thought she wouldn't like you if you didn't fit into the realm of what she might want. Did you even try to win her over without going through all of this trouble?"

He cocked his head to the side and his eyes flickered with something strange. His focus swept over her face from the top of her head to her mouth and then bounced back to her eyes. "But if I hadn't decided to do that, then you wouldn't have someone to work on your mother's truck. In a way, you should be thanking her."

"Okay, yeah. I'll make sure to do that next time." She snorted and moved to finish brushing Blaze down when Adam stopped her.

"You wanna know what I think?"

"What do you think?" Her voice hitched, giving herself away.

"I think you're jealous."

Her mouth dry, all she could do was stare at him. There they were, confined to a small stall in the barn. She was all but pinned between him and the horse behind her. Yes, if she wanted to, she could slip beneath Blaze's belly and move to the other side.

Only she didn't want to.

Not in the slightest.

Her head told her to make her escape. This wasn't in the plan. He'd cornered her like the little mouse she was, and this wouldn't bode well for either of them.

But her heart, the rebel that it was, refused.

"So what if I am?"

His brow lifted.

Time stopped. Everything slowed except for her heart and her racing pulse. Wrong. This was all wrong. She shook her head and held up her hands between them, though due to lack of space, they ended up resting on his chest. "You have a girlfriend."

"I told you, she's not my girlfriend."

"You were on a *date* with her."

He tucked his finger under her chin and gently lifted her face, her gaze moving to his eyes before he spoke again. "No, we weren't."

She blinked. "You weren't?" Her mouth had gone completely dry. She couldn't swallow if she wanted to. Adam had managed to blindside her for a second time that day and she was struggling to keep up.

Adam's gaze dipped to her mouth. "And I *really* want to kiss you."

That did it. All rationality and common sense fled from her body. With one whispered word, she doomed herself. "Okay."

16

———

Adam

dam's eyes searched hers back and forth.

It can't be this easy.

Of course it can. She literally gave you permission.

Kiss the girl before she changes her mind, you numbskull.

He tilted her chin upward a fraction and slowly lowered his lips to brush against hers. A strange hum buzzed between them. Or maybe it was a purring sound like that of a well-oiled engine. The connection was intoxicating, making him feel like he had taken drugs of some kind.

Adam had kissed women before. He'd had his fair share of relationships.

But this was different.

This was... electrifying.

Faye breathed life into him with her scent and her beautiful eyes. She kept him on his toes with her sharp tongue and quick wit.

She had more talent in one finger than most had in their whole body, and he should have noticed long before now.

And she wanted him.

At least that's what he told himself as he allowed his hands to frame her face so he could feel her soft skin. This kiss hinted at something far greater and incomprehensible than he would have ever dreamed possible.

She was like putty in his hands, soft and yet firm, willing to be molded and shaped into what he needed. That wasn't to say he wanted to change her. It was that she fit every single thing on his list, and he'd been blind to it.

A soft moan left her lips, shattering his thoughts and bringing him back to reality. Adam pulled back reluctantly, wishing this kiss didn't have to end but knowing that wasn't a possibility.

Her eyes opened, clear as the summer sky.

Now what?

Do something, quick, or she's going to push you away.

She wouldn't do that.

Were you not there the last time she got mad? This one is a fireball.

But she's going to be my fireball.

He grinned at her, tracing her jawline with the edge of his thumb. "That was…" There were literally no words he could say to express how happy she'd made him feel. And if there were, he'd never heard them before. "Please tell me you felt it."

Her lips parted and she exhaled.

Chills rocketed through him. She didn't have to speak. He'd seen what pushing her could do, and right now, he was content just to be this close to her and have her permission to touch her in this intimate way. Was he crazy?

No. This was something else entirely.

Not love. He wouldn't go so far as to jump off *that* cliff.

But something was brewing, and it was big.

"Don't say anything if you don't want to. I'm fine with that. You can think about this, and we can talk about it again later."

"When?" Her whisper was soft, but it had the strength alone to lift the hairs on the back of his neck.

"Whenever you're ready." He stepped back, forcing himself to give her the distance she needed when all he wanted was to pull her into his arms and claim her for his own. "I mean it. Whenever you want to talk, I'll be here." Adam put his thumb over his shoulder. "But I should probably get going." He didn't want to jinx this moment.

"What about Dahlia?"

"What about her?"

"Are you two... Is she...?"

He reached for her hands. "She was a crush. That wasn't even an official date."

"What does that make me?"

"Whatever you want to be." He closed the distance between them once more and pressed a kiss to her forehead, then he darted out of that barn like his tail was on fire. He probably looked like a crazed lunatic the way he shot from the building and headed straight for his truck. It was for the best, not only for Faye but for himself as well.

ADAM COULDN'T FOCUS on work for the entire week. He'd promised himself he'd give her space to think about what had happened between them, and that was exactly what he was going to do.

Only, he'd expected to hear from her at least once. But he got no text messages or phone calls. This could very well be a sign that she wasn't interested. He'd moved too quickly. He shouldn't have kissed her.

Adam let out a big sigh as he leaned against the wall of his garage. This was bad. Worse than bad. He'd put himself out there with no plan, no fail-safe. He hadn't had a plan. What did he think he could do? Just go from putting the two of them in the friend zone to being in a romantic position?

Yeah. That *always* worked out for other guys.

And then there was his competition.

It didn't matter that Faye said this Wade guy wasn't in the picture. For all Adam knew, he hadn't said any such thing. There was a good chance of a love triangle between Faye, her sister, and this intimidating cowboy.

"We've got another one." Bridget moved past him toward the garage door and pulled it up. Her chin grazed her shoulder as she looked back at him. "You okay?"

"Fine," he muttered. "What do we have?"

She didn't believe him. Well, that didn't matter. They were coworkers, not buddies.

The driver of the vehicle they'd be working on pulled into the garage, and Bridget let the large metal garage door roll closed. Her eyes didn't leave Adam as he wandered over to their customer. He could feel her watchful gaze which made listening to the owner of the vehicle a little harder.

When their customer exited the building, Adam spun around, his arms crossed. "What?"

She shrugged, shaking her head. The expression on her face was probably supposed to appear innocent, but he didn't buy that for a second. Adam moved toward her, holding out his finger. "You know something, don't you?"

Once again, she shook her head. "Nope. I've just watched you slowly get a little lazier, and I wanted to know what I needed to do in order to get things back on track. This is kinda getting ridiculous."

"I'm not lazy."

"Fine, distracted. I get it. Something is going on with you at home. Maybe it's something with your family, maybe it's a girl. But you need to figure out how to leave it at home."

His brows creased. Bridget was the furthest thing from a typical mechanic. He'd been surprised when he came home to find her working for his dad. First of all, she was a girl. Not many women chose this profession. It wasn't that they weren't completely capable of such a job; it was that most of them didn't like getting grease under their fingernails.

At least, that was how he saw it.

She was a girl, though.

His focus followed her as she walked around the truck to the driver's side and pulled the door open. With a click, the hood popped up. It would be unprofessional to ask for her advice. They'd kept their distance from such things. But then again, if she'd noticed his work ethic suffering, perhaps she wouldn't mind lending her opinions on this subject.

"It's nothing at home."

Bridget was leaning into the engine, checking the hoses with a gloved hand. She glanced up at him then back to the engine. "That's good for you, I guess."

"It's not even bad."

"*Okay*. That's good too."

Boy, he was butchering this. He should have figured out a way to phrase this in his mind before trying to speak to her about it. Now he not only looked incompetent, he probably sounded like a fool. "How long have you been with Travis?"

She stilled, then slowly she climbed out of where she'd managed to put herself. "So it *is* a girl."

He shook his head, his eyes closed. "It doesn't matter. I just want to ask a few questions."

"Okay, I've been with him for a couple years, I guess."

"When things first started out, were you guys talking all the time?"

Bridget cocked her head and placed a hand on her hip. "I don't understand where you're getting at with this line of questioning."

"Were you talking every day? Seeing each other frequently."

"Sure. I mean, I was hanging out with his sister a lot, and of course, he'd be around because of her. What does that have to do with—"

"You're a girl."

She laughed. "Yes, that would be accurate."

"I kissed this woman on Saturday. And it's Friday. She hasn't messaged me or called. I wanted to give her time to think over what happened, but I'm on edge because now I feel like this lack of communication could only mean one thing."

"Ooh. Yeah. That doesn't sound good. She hasn't responded to any of your texts?"

"I haven't messaged her."

This time Bridget tossed her head back and laughed loud enough that it echoed in the shop. "Well, why not?"

"I already told you."

"I don't care about that. You kissed her, then you walked away. Now you're wondering why she isn't *messaging* you? Buddy, she's not messaging you because you threw her a curve ball. She doesn't want to be the first one to reach out."

"But I'm the one who kissed *her*. Doesn't that mean she should be the one to tell me what it means?"

Bridget rolled her eyes. "She's probably trying to figure out the same thing. What if she's wondering if this is a fluke? She might be talking herself out of ever seeing you again—"

"That's not gonna happen."

"Oh yeah? Sounds like someone has a bit too much confidence if you ask me."

Adam gestured toward Faye's mother's truck which had taken up one of the bays for the last month and a half. "She has to come get that at some point."

Bridget's eyes bounced to the truck then back to his face. The only way he could describe her expression was that it was one of pity. "Oh, *Adam.* Is that why you offered free labor? You were trying to impress her? Wait, you *kissed* her? Well, if she's not shown any interest in you this far, I doubt—"

"It wasn't like that." He let out a groan and dragged his hand down his face. This wasn't how this conversation was supposed to go. She was supposed to tell him that Faye was just taking her time and she'd get back to him when she was ready. Now he didn't know if he should have been touching base with her all this time.

They were in the modern century. It shouldn't be this hard.

"So I call her—text her—whatever. Then what?"

Bridget's smile still ate at him. He hated the way she was making him feel like he'd messed everything up with just one look. And maybe he had. There was no telling how everything would go from this point forward. He didn't even know if he could fix this.

Bridget leaned her hip against the truck. She studied him, her eyes seemingly able to read his thoughts which made his brain itch. "No. Don't text her. Don't call. You've waited all week long, and if I were her and I hadn't heard from you, I would assume you weren't as interested as you may have made it seem."

"But I *am*—"

"Doesn't matter if you are or aren't at this point. You are *both* to her, and you've let her stew all week long about what that kiss might have meant. If you want my advice, I'd go see her tonight and take her on a walk or a picnic... something where you can tell her how you feel."

"That's just it. I don't know how I feel."

She arched a brow. "Really." Her voice was flat and assumed far too much. "You've clearly developed feelings for her. Otherwise, you wouldn't be doing such a terrible job around here."

His mouth dropped open, and he just about started a rant regarding how much he did around here, but she stopped him.

"You might not have those deep feelings yet. But you're thinking about her constantly and you *want* something to happen, right?"

"I suppose you're right."

"Well, that's enough then. Ask her out on an official date and tell her that you want to see where things might go. If she says she wants the same thing, then you're golden. If she says no, then at least you have your answer."

As simple as that seemed, it terrified him.

"Only, I'd send her a quick message so you don't just show up and find out she's with another guy."

His head whipped around and he stared at her.

She chuckled, turning her attention back to the truck. "Relax. It's going to work out. These things usually do."

"Shouldn't I just wait until tomorrow to see her? That's when we usually get together. I could message her and ask if she's coming to work on the truck—"

Bridget laughed again. "What are you so afraid of? Seriously. This is a girl we're talking about. It's not like you have to talk to her father. Now, Zeke Callahan isn't the kind of guy I'd want to have a meeting with." She let out a low whistle. Her hand on her hip, she tilted her head once more. "Just bite the bullet and tell her you want to see her tonight. Then maybe you can actually get some quality work done around here."

17

Faye

Faye's stomach had been in a constant state of upheaval since the last time she saw Adam. Her sisters had all called her crazy at one point or another but meant it in different ways. Those who were married or involved with a guy told her to just rip off the Band-Aid and go see him. There wasn't any reason for her to sit and stew about where their relationship was headed.

Basically, they told her to put herself out of her misery.

Then there was Brielle and Eloise. The only other sisters who couldn't care less about dating anyone seriously. Brielle had even suggested that she go out tonight to the country club and find a random guy to pull in for a kiss.

That wasn't a helpful suggestion. And she had a sinking suspicion that Brielle was only telling Faye to do so to get back at her for bringing Wade by the house. That was an issue all on its own.

If Brielle didn't want the guy to inquire about her, she shouldn't have flirted with him. It was her own fault.

So now Faye stewed on her front porch debating about whether she should get ready to go dancing with Eloise and Brielle, go for a ride to clear her head, or just call the guy and tell him he was a jerk for kissing her and then running away like a big coward.

Nope.

She wasn't going to do that last one. Faye Callahan wasn't the kind of girl to go chasing after a guy who didn't want to be with her. Adam might have kissed her and said some really romantic things, but if he wasn't going to stick around, then he clearly was doing and saying those things for show.

Faye jumped up from her chair then paused. She still hadn't decided whether she was going for that ride or going out with her sisters. If she went to the club, she very well could run into Adam. Or worse, she could run into Dahlia.

A horse ride it was.

She'd just get her boots, hat, phone, and...

And there was a truck coming up the road to her house. Her heart flipped like a glorified acrobat performing a trick on the trapeze. She knew that truck. What was Adam doing here?

Faye glanced toward the house and then the barn. Yes, she was looking for an escape. Had he contacted her even once before today, she might have been able to handle it. The problem was, she'd built up the expectation for this conversation so high in her head that she didn't think she could stomach it now.

As much as she wanted to dart inside and tell her sisters that she wasn't home, she couldn't. Her feet wouldn't move.

Shoot!

There was a part of her that wanted to put him in his place, and that part of her was ready to see the fallout. Instead of moving toward the house, her feet took her to the edge of the porch. She crossed her arms and waited for him to get out of his truck.

Faye didn't know what she was going to say to him. Her feet and her heart had a mind of their own, and they'd have to come up with something.

Adam climbed out of his truck. He left his door open and leaned against it as his eyes locked with hers. They stood there like they were posing for a painting. He didn't say anything, and she still hadn't come up with anything she could say to him.

A smile tugged at his lips, which only made her insides spin out of control. Yep, she should have gone inside when she had the chance.

He pushed the door closed and then sauntered toward her. As much as she wanted to throw a well-deserved snarky comment in his direction, she couldn't. Her eyes followed him as he approached right up until he reached the foot of the stairs.

Faye shook her head. "You have a lot of nerve coming here without so much as a phone call or a text message."

Adam's infuriating smile widened. He rested his elbow on the railing and gazed up at her with amusement. "You didn't get it?"

"Get what? The message you failed to send?"

He chuckled. "You don't have any idea what you've put me through this week."

"What *I've* put you through? What about you? What kind of guy just goes and kisses a girl like that and then doesn't even explain himself?"

Adam put a foot up on the bottom step.

"Don't you dare." It was the only thing she could think of to tell him, and those words were enough to make her blush bright red. If he had the capability to read her mind, he would have been a witness to the way he affected her. Every internal mechanism that operated her body had gone haywire.

"You really didn't get my message?"

Her brows shot up. "Wait, you really messaged me?"

He nodded slowly and her blush intensified.

"What did it say?"

Adam laughed. "I wanted to know if you'd go out with me."

Faye stared at him, not knowing what to say. There was a large part of her that had wanted him to do this very thing at the beginning of the week. She'd picked up her phone several times over the last week just to see if she'd missed something from him. It wasn't until today that she'd allowed her walls to come up. "But you have a girlfriend."

A groan escaped his lips. Instead of an eye roll, his whole body shifted and rolled. He let out a strained laugh. "First of all, she's not my girlfriend."

"But you wanted her to be."

He raked a hand through his hair then shook his head. His frustration was getting to him, and she could see it more clearly than before. She almost felt guilty over what she was doing to him. Adam climbed two steps then paused. "Do you know how hard it was for me to come here this evening? You have *any idea* the torture I've been dealing with this past week thinking that you had *zero* interest in me?"

Faye opened her mouth, but no words came out. He moved closer still, and all she could do was watch him close the distance between them and pray her weak legs continued to hold her up. She faced him when he got to the landing. "To be fair, I was waiting for you to call me."

He clicked his tongue. "I distinctly remember telling you that I was ready to talk about this whenever you were."

Her eyes widened, the realization hitting her like a bus. He was right. He'd told her that right before he left. How had she managed to forget that part of their first kiss? Faye had been so consumed with the kiss itself that she'd blocked out everything else. She dropped her hands to her sides. "Oh."

Well, this was just great. She'd spent the whole week wondering what he was thinking when she could have been the one to reach out and ask him to coffee or something. Now she was beyond embarrassed and didn't even know why he'd come.

Adam reached for her hand and traced his thumb over her knuckles back and forth. Chills raced down her spine from his touch. If she could have done the week over, she would have called.

"I'm sorry," she blurted. "You're right. I should have called and let you know..." Let him know what exactly? She'd been so consumed with trying to figure out that very thing that she didn't have an answer for him.

"You don't have to be sorry. I could have just as easily stopped over here." That was true.

"Why exactly did you come over then? I didn't respond. What if I didn't want to talk to you?"

His lips quirked upward and he edged closer. "That was a risk I was willing to take."

The way his voice tickled her senses and his smile made her toes want to curl was unlike anything she'd ever experienced before. This was a crush. That's all it was. But at the same time, it felt like so much more. She couldn't put her finger on why she knew in her heart this was the path she wanted to take.

Adam continued. "Well, that, and Bridget told me if I didn't come out here and get it off my chest, then she was going to quit."

Faye laughed. "You're kidding."

He grimaced. "Unfortunately, not."

"Well, what did you want to get off your chest?"

Dropping his gaze once more, Adam shifted in front of her. "I suppose we've cleared most of it already. I just haven't outright said what I want. But then, neither have you. This whole time you've been teaching me about horses, and I've been teaching you a little bit about cars. But somewhere along the way, that changed—at least for me." He lifted his gaze, locking it with hers. "It's like I said, I came here to ask you out. *You*, Faye—I'm not interested in anyone else. But I need to know if you feel the same way. I'm not interested in a pity date or one where you feel you don't really have a choice."

She lifted a single brow. "Have you *met* my father?"

That smile appeared just as readily as it had before. "You make a good point." He glanced toward the house and made a face. "He's not standing behind that door with a shotgun, is he?"

Faye laughed. "No. But don't think he won't. From what I recall, he did that exact thing when Adeline and Sean got together."

He lifted his brows.

"It's a whole thing." She waved her hand dismissively. "So what's the plan? I assume you have one."

Adam shrugged. "I just wanted to spend some time with you—outside of our usual arrangement. That's still on for tomorrow, by the way. I have all the parts set up and ready to go."

"Then what are we going to do tonight?"

"Well, Bridget seemed to think a picnic would be a good idea."

"She's pretty smart." Faye didn't know if it was the way he was still holding her hand or if it was due to the fact that they'd both lowered their voices, but she edged even closer to him. Any closer and their bodies would press up against one another. That wouldn't be so bad. She might get a second kiss from him.

Adam must have thought the same thing. While his lips continued to hold that heart-dropping smile, his face dipped closer and his voice dropped to just above a whisper. "I think so. That's why I brought one."

Her eyes widened. "Really?"

"I figured I had to do something to win you over in case you really were trying to avoid me."

She looked past him to his truck. "What did you bring?"

"Some sandwiches, fruit, chips... you know, the usual stuff."

"I don't believe it."

He straightened, his brows creasing with confusion. "I would never lie to you, Faye."

A soft laugh slipped out. "I wasn't suggesting you were lying. I just can't believe a guy would go to so much trouble for... well, for me."

A myriad of emotions flitted across his face. "Why not?'

She shrugged. "I've never had a guy interested in me before."

"I doubt that."

Faye tugged her hand from his and gestured around them. "Oh, right. Because there are *so* many suitors surrounding us."

He captured her hand and brought it to his lips, success-fully ending her sarcastic comment. "One thing you're going to learn pretty quickly is that guys as a breed are pretty igno-rant about women. We have very few talents, and knowing how to talk to a girl we like isn't usually one of them. I'm just lucky that none of them have been brave enough to sweep you off your feet—like that Wade guy."

She bit back a smile. The fact that he'd brought up Wade again meant he really thought the guy was a threat or he was jealous. Perhaps it was both.

Adam took a step back, tugging on her hand and pulling her toward the steps.

"Oh. So we're going right now?"

"Do you have anywhere else you need to be?"

That was the question of the century. It was a Friday night. Of course she didn't have anywhere else she needed to be. She was just taken off guard. For once in her life, she had the opportunity to fly by the seat of her pants and throw caution out the window.

Would it be a mistake to accept Adam's invitation? Maybe. But right now, she didn't see any reason not to.

She allowed him to guide her to his truck, where he opened the door for her. "I have the perfect place," he murmured. "Hang tight and I'll show you where I like to go."

Faye watched him jog around the front of the truck before he climbed behind the steering wheel. He flashed her a crooked grin and started the engine. Then he reached for her left hand and laced his fingers with hers.

She stared down where they were connected and marveled, not for the first time, at how well their hands fit together. If this was what all her sisters felt with the men in their lives, no wonder why they were pushing her to just jump in with eyes shut tight. This felt amazing. It was like she'd finally found the one thing that had been missing from her life.

It wasn't her mother's truck. It wasn't a job.

It was someone she could belong to.

And his name was Adam.

18

Adam

$\mathcal{A}$dam couldn't believe how right Bridget was. How could it have been this simple? He had never shied away from anything in his life until he started viewing Faye in a different way.

He peeked at her out of the corner of his eye and a thrill rocketed through him. He'd been expecting her to tell him off, to never see her again.

Though he didn't know how that would work, considering the truck still needed quite a bit of work.

All of those thoughts fell by the wayside now that he had her hand in his. He was going to do this right. He'd woo her until she couldn't stand to be away from him. And the best part was that he already knew her, and she knew him—a relationship he didn't share with Dahlia.

He squeezed her hand, and she glanced at him. His heart raced as he considered what this could mean for his future.

Adam had come back to Copper Creek to help his father out. He'd resigned himself to running the auto shop mostly because he wanted to keep it in the family. The fact that his father hadn't asked him to come back in so many words was enough proof that he probably didn't care if the place was run by family.

Bridget could have been just as good of a choice.

But now he felt he had a real reason to seriously put down roots.

What was this feeling?

Euphoria?

They hadn't even been on an official date, and he couldn't stop smiling. All the stress from the past week washed away.

Yes, it was that easy.

Adam pulled into the parking lot for the shop and Faye shifted in her seat. She bent forward and peered out the front window. "Did you forget something at work?"

He shook his head. "Nope." The confusion that filtered across her face only added to his excitement. "I can honestly say I have never brought anyone here before. It's kind of like that place you took me to when we went riding."

She turned toward him and he could read the understanding in her expression. He hoped his statement hit home for her.

"I know it's weird, but you have to see it to know what I'm talking about."

Her mouth twitched. "I'm sorry, Adam, I fail to see how an auto body shop can be romantic." Faye snapped her mouth shut and her eyes widened but only for a moment. "Unless it's not supposed to be romantic. I don't want to assume—"

"Just come inside with me." Adam kissed her hand once more before relinquishing it and stepping from the truck. First, he opened the back door and reached for the handles of the large wicker picnic basket. Then he hurried around to get Faye's door for her, only to find she'd opened the door on her own.

He frowned but didn't point out that he wanted her to be treated like a princess tonight and part of that was him doing stuff like this for her. Adam shut the door before holding out his hand. This time she accepted his offering without a second thought. The action had become second nature to both of them, and he couldn't deny how much that fact thrilled him.

Adam leaned closer to her as they wandered toward the front door. "So we're going to have to be here for a few hours before it's really gonna get good, but that will give us enough time to eat."

Faye let out a laugh. "You realize you sound ridiculous, right? This place is covered in grease and dirt. I bet it smells like rubber and oil. If you can convince me that this place holds even a degree of romance, I'll kiss you on the spot."

He stopped suddenly and the action caused her to jerk backward due to her hand still being caught in his own. "Is that a promise?"

She met his gaze, and the tension that grew between them was so thick he could have cut through it with a dull blade. Her lashes fluttered when she blinked a few times and her cheeks filled with a pretty pink color. "Sure. That's what I said, wasn't it?"

"I just want a guarantee that you'll make good on your promises. Because if you think your little cliff is the place that beats all, just wait until you get a look at what I'm going to show you."

Faye rolled her eyes, but the smile returned, nevertheless. "Okay, Mr. Romantic. Prove it. Show me what makes this place so amazing that you have never brought anyone here." She snickered and Adam grasped her hand a little tighter. He couldn't wait to show her exactly what he was talking about.

"How about you give me an appetizer to whet my appetite?" He tapped his cheek but didn't expect her to do anything about it.

Then she did.

In two short steps she stood before him, her wide eyes peering up into his and her pretty mouth pursed together. "You think you've earned a kiss?"

He swallowed hard, unable to bring himself to utter a single word.

Her voice lowered to a seductive level, or maybe that was all in his head and it was just a whisper. "I'll kiss you, but if you don't make good on your promise, what do I get?"

"A picnic?" he rasped.

She lifted her hand to his cheek. The warmth of her skin pressing against his did crazy things to his insides. She stood on her toes, and for a second, his excitement exploded as he thought she'd be kissing him full on the mouth.

Only she didn't. Her lips brushed tenderly along his jaw before she stopped right at the place where he'd pointed. She pulled back just far enough to meet his gaze. The temptation to grab her right there and claim her lips for himself was too great. He needed a distraction. His hand tightened around the basket handles, wicker digging into his palm. "Like I said," he rasped. "You're going to have to be patient. We have to wait for the best part. But until then, I'll show you what I've got."

Faye patted his cheek, and just like that, the bubble of tension popped. She withdrew from him and flounced toward the door, looking over her shoulder once, presumably to see if he was coming.

He sucked in a deep breath that seemed to fill his lungs all the way down to his stomach. Adam didn't know what he'd gotten himself into. He only knew that he loved it.

They entered the shop and not a sound welcomed them. He'd closed up right before he'd driven out to meet Faye. They had the place to themselves.

Faye slowed her steps once they were in the waiting area. She clearly had no idea what he had up his sleeve, and that notion filled him with more joy than anything else could have. Adam jerked his chin toward the shop, and she wrinkled her nose.

"I don't think so."

"What? Don't you trust me?"

She laughed. "That's where cars either go to die or you bring them back to life. There is nothing in there I want to see, I can assure you."

He chuckled. "Come on. It's not haunted or anything."

Faye stopped suddenly, causing him to bump into her. "Wait, it's haunted?"

"*No*, I said it *wasn't* haunted. But if we take too long talking about it, then we're going to miss out on everything I wanted to show you. Come on. Don't fight me so hard on this." Adam moved past her, opening the door to where they worked on the cars all day. His gaze landed on Faye's mother's truck, and he shot a look over his shoulder toward Faye.

She sent him a confused look. "Why did you move it to the middle bay?"

"You'll see." He motioned for her to follow him, and when they got to the back of the truck, he pulled down the tailgate. "Climb in. I have to get something."

Faye stared at him like he was crazy, which only made him laugh again.

"Seriously. You're gonna have to trust me. It's not that hard, you know. Certainly not as hard as learning how to ride a horse for the rodeo." Adam nodded to the bed of the truck one final time. "Go on."

She shook her head. "If you're planning something that shouldn't be happening, you realize that my father's shotgun will be in your future, right?" Without further argument, she climbed into the bed and tugged the basket near her.

He headed toward a workbench on the far side of the shop, his hands rummaging through the supplies he had piled there until he found the small black object he was looking for. As swift as he'd made it to the bench, he returned to her side.

Adam closed the tailgate then climbed inside. "Okay, we're going to have our food, and then I'm going to show you what makes this place special."

A sigh burst from her lips while amusement danced in her gaze. "I get it, Adam. This truck is special because it was my mother's. And as sweet as you were to think of me and bring me here to have a picnic in the back of her truck—"

"That's not what makes this special," he insisted. "It's more than that. You're just going to have to be *patient*." Adam wasn't about to let her make a mess of things. He fully intended on showing her the time of her life, and it all started in the back of this truck.

Plates were filled with food and red solo cups held the sparkling cider he'd packed. Faye kept looking over at him, then when he caught her staring, she'd look away.

"You really haven't brought *anyone* here before?"

He chewed his sandwich thoughtfully. "You know, I don't think it ever occurred to me before you took me to your favorite place. I mean, I always assumed that something like this would happen with my future wife. I guess I never connected the fact that I'd need to have a first date and then get married to make that happen."

She glanced around the shop. "Yeah, because power tools, hoses, and other broken-down vehicles are *so* romantic."

"You really should give me the benefit of the doubt. You're going to feel so sheepish when you realize that you're wrong."

Faye had gone from stiff and suspicious of him to playing along with him. He could already tell she had relaxed. Excitement came off her in waves. That light he loved about her had returned, and he found himself growing giddy due to what the rest of the evening held.

Without warning her, he pressed on the small black remote he'd grabbed from the work bench. The hydraulic system beneath them whirred to life and the truck lurched upward.

Faye gasped. Her hands flew outward to grasp onto something, but there wasn't anything for her to hold. They weren't going terribly fast, but the surprise had done its job. Eyes wide, Faye edged over to the side of the bed and looked down. "Should we even be in here? What happens if we get stuck? Is there a way down?"

"*Relax.*" He laughed. "This machinery can hold twice the weight of your truck at least. We'll be fine. Just don't try to make some grand escape while we're up here, okay?"

She shot him a dirty look, but her tone still held that teasing sarcasm he was beginning to realize was her way of flirting. "Oh, so *that's* why you brought me here—so I won't escape."

He shook his head. "You really are something, you know? I thought women were supposed to be mild and sweet, but you're...."

The expression on her face darkened. This one wasn't teasing at all. "I'm what?"

"You're amazing."

She blinked. "What?"

"Yeah. You know what you want. You figure out how to get it. You don't need *anyone* to fulfill you. It's like you have this streak of independence. You wouldn't stick around if you didn't *want* to. That's probably why I was so nervous all week." He forced a smile. "It's thrilling, really."

Adam tore his gaze away from her. The way she was looking at him made him feel exposed. He didn't know what prompted him to tell her any of that. He wasn't even sure where those words came from. It was as if some outside force had put them in his mouth so he could understand and feel some semblance of security.

If he didn't mess this up, Faye might stick around for the long haul.

The sun was going down, making the shop darker—something even Faye had noticed. It wasn't lost on him that she hadn't commented on his description of her. She didn't need to, of course. The lack of comment was enough for him to know she wanted to let it settle.

Instead, she adjusted the way she sat so her legs crossed beneath her. "What do we do now? Do you have a candle or something? Does that little remote in your hand turn on lights?"

Adam shook his head. "No lights. It's going to be at least another half hour. But I do have a few candles." He chanced a look in her direction, finding that the smile had returned to her face. "Do you trust me?"

Faye tilted her head, her grin spreading. Then she pulled her lower lip between her teeth. Her eyes swept around them, landing on him, their picnic, and the shop that surrounded them. "Okay. I trust you."

He would never get used to the thrill that filled him when

everything started to fall into place. Faye was here with him, and in less than an hour, he'd be able to share the one thing he hadn't shared with anyone. This was his moment to shine —to show her he was worth it.

19

Faye

Faye was a bundle of nerves. She probably should be terrified right now, but the only thing she felt was elation. She was a romantic; that much was clear. This whole date was more than she could have dreamed. It was unique—special.

Some part of her knew that Adam was special. Way back when he'd admitted to wanting to learn riding to impress a girl, she could see that he was more thoughtful than the average guy who lived in Copper Creek. Adam didn't just take her to coffee. He didn't ask surface questions that inevitably ended in them not connecting at all.

No, Adam was the kind of guy who thought outside of the box.

She caught herself staring at him far too many times as darkness descended around them. They were so high up, and she probably should have been worried about how they'd go about getting down without the lights on. But for some reason being here with him could make all those cares go away.

Faye grasped her cup with both hands and took a sip as she eyed Adam over the rim. It was quiet, but not uncomfortably so. Funny how she could be with him like this and not feel awkward. Her thoughts bounced from idea to idea until she landed on something she was genuinely curious about. "I guess this means you're not going to continue trying to learn the ways of the rodeo?"

He shrugged. "I don't know. I've really enjoyed what I've been learning. It might be fun to still try for something like that."

She bit back a frown. Culturally speaking, the folks out here enjoyed the rodeo. They liked watching cowboys ride and rope with accuracy. They could enjoy the various competitions without thinking too much about what was happening to the animals or how the men risked their lives.

But there was a reason her father had never shown an interest in competing or let his daughters get into it. Aspects of the sport were definitely dangerous. On top of worrying about his safety, she couldn't help but think about his reasons for trying the rodeo in the first place. He wanted to impress Dahlia, right? She ran in those circles, and by the way Dahlia had been looking at Adam when they'd all bumped into each other at the country club, Faye wouldn't be surprised if the woman was interested in him.

A trickle of jealousy ate at her, but she quickly shoved those thoughts aside. Adam was here with her, not Dahlia. She needed to live in the moment, enjoy what he had planned.

She took another sip of her drink then placed the cup down. She could now only see his face from the flickering light of the candle.

He cocked his head as he leaned back and put all his weight on the palm of his hand. "Why do you ask? Are you tired of teaching me?"

Faye could tell him now. It would be easy to explain her opinions of the dangers involved with the rodeo. Doing so meant she might ruin their evening. That conversation could come another time when they were riding. She shook her head. "I enjoy our rides far too much to stop teaching you. Besides, you still have a ton to learn."

He scoffed. "Excuse me? I think I do a pretty good job of holding my own."

"I don't think they'd let you enter the rodeo with a horse like Bella." She giggled. "If you're serious about the rodeo, you're going to have to do a lot more than learn how to handle a horse. You're going to have to learn how to handle a specific kind of horse."

It was too dark to tell if he was amused right along with her or if he didn't like what she had told him. He didn't respond, only bent to pick up a few things and put them back in the basket.

She straightened. "Are we ready? Is it happening?"

Adam grinned then reached for the candle to her right. He held it closer to his face and she could see the reflection of the flame in his eyes. "We're ready." He took a deep breath and then puffed the flame out.

Everything around her was black and she blinked several times to help her eyes adjust to the dark. That's when she realized they were glowing. She lifted her arms then looked up and gasped. There were two large skylights overhead that she'd never noticed before.

Faye dropped her gaze to where Adam was seated beside her. He handed her a blanket and then spread his out before lying atop of it. His hands clasped behind his head, and he chuckled. "Well, come on. You're going to miss it."

"Miss what?" She dropped the blanket beside his and settled onto her back to stare up at the skylight. They were a lot closer than she'd realized. It was like they had their own personal window to the heavens.

He brought down his hands from behind his head and they rested between the two of them. His small finger brushed against hers, sending her heart into erratic flurries. Faye bit back a giddy grin. She couldn't bring herself to look at him, so she kept her eyes trained on the stars that had begun to shine through the skylight. "I would have thought it was too bright to see stars around here. I mean, out at my family's ranch, you can see *everything*."

Adam twisted his head around and she finally turned toward him. "I shut off the outside lights. And it certainly helps that we're a smaller town than Colorado Springs." He shifted as if he needed to get comfortable, then he lifted his hand and pointed toward the window. "See that brighter star in the upper right corner of the window?"

Faye followed his direction. "Yeah."

"That one's mine."

She snorted. "What? Did you adopt it or something?"

He didn't answer right away, which caused her to turn her head toward him once again. He smiled. "When I was eight, I had a thing for stars."

Stunned, she didn't know what to say. Not only was Adam sensitive, but he also had an appreciation for nature, and he knew how to work on cars. He was a boyfriend trifecta. She couldn't believe he hadn't gotten married by now.

Adam chuckled. "What?"

His word tore her from her frozen state. She blinked and let out a laugh of her own. "You were a nerd."

"*Hey!*" He dropped his hand between them again, but this time he reached for her hand. His fingers laced between hers. The connection sent a ripple of pleasant shivers through her body.

"So, what did you name it?"

He stiffened. She couldn't see it, but there was just something about the air between them.

Faye scooted a little closer to him. "What did you name your star?"

"I don't want to say."

She sat up on her elbow with a laugh. "It can't be that bad. It's a star. You were a kid. What did you name your little star?"

His eyes shifted to her then returned to the window. "Atom."

Faye let out a laugh. "Adam? You named your star after you?"

He shook his head. "A-tom. But yeah. I named it after me. I thought it'd be funny that people would pronounce the names the same."

She dropped down again and stared at the sky. "I think it's sweet. Cute little Adam naming a star so it sounds like his name." Without really thinking about it, she snuggled next to him. Their view of the sky was about the size of a large flat-screen television, but it was enough to give the right romantic effect. Her cheek rested against his shoulder, and he turned his head to kiss her temple.

Goosebumps lifted on her arms and she trembled.

"You cold?"

"No," she murmured. There was no way she was going to tell him just how much he affected her. This was the start of something new—something great—something she wouldn't take for granted.

ONE MONTH later

Faye watched Adam as he hunched over the hood of his latest and tightened something or loosened something. At this point she didn't know what he was doing or how she was supposed to be helping. All she wanted to do was admire him as he did what he did best.

Adam lifted his head and gave her that crooked grin that turned her legs into mush. "You gonna make yourself useful, or are you going to just stand there?"

"I *am* being useful."

He straightened, putting the tool in his hand down on a nearby table. He grabbed a dirty rag from his shoulder to clean his hands before tossing it back there again. Leaning his hip against the truck, he grinned at her. "How is that? By eating my snacks and taking up all the oxygen?" Adam sauntered closer then tugged her toward him. "Because that doesn't seem very helpful to me."

She tilted her head as she draped her arms around his neck. "I keep you company. Isn't that enough? This isn't even my mom's truck, which by the way, we finished last week."

"*We?*" He tossed his head back and laughed. "From what I recall, you haven't lifted a finger since our first official date. But you *have* provided me with something pretty to look at."

Pleasure coursed through her body at his compliment. She still hadn't gotten used to the way he talked about her in that way. She'd assumed that this honeymoon phase of their relationship would quickly die off, but as of now there was no end in sight.

Adam lowered his mouth to capture hers in a breath-stealing kiss that made her toes curl. He swung her around and stared into her eyes, lighting her insides on fire.

Over the last month, they'd gone from seeing each other every weekend to spending every spare moment together. He'd been getting better at riding, but much to his disappointment, she'd lost interest in working on anything mechanical—though she couldn't help but love watching him work.

Faye turned her head to the side to catch her breath. Being with Adam was easy—like breathing. They got along so well it was hard to believe.

"Ahem."

She gasped, pushing Adam away from her with a force she didn't know she had.

He took a stumbled step backward, and for a moment, she worried he'd lose his balance. Adam turned toward their intrusion just as Faye looked up. Bridget eyed them with amusement. She had one hand on her hip and the other holding a stack of mail. "You know, there are better places to make out—with more privacy."

Faye's cheeks flooded with heat. It was easy being with Adam except when they were caught together. There was one thing that she had a hard time with. It was strange, but she never thought she'd actually be scared to fully *commit*. A whole month and she still hadn't called him her boyfriend, nor had they had *the talk*.

Was she seeing anyone else? No. And she was fairly certain he wasn't dating anyone else. But to put a label on it just felt impossible. It was better to be easy—to go with the flow.

She shoved her hands into her pockets and looked at her feet. It would be naïve to believe no one noticed how much time they spent together. The town probably had given them the exact label she was avoiding taking for herself.

They had time. There was no need to rush this.

Bridget held out the stack of papers. "Mail came. Thought

you might want it. Looks like you got that informational packet about the rodeo coming to Colorado Springs."

Faye's ears perked up. Adam hadn't mentioned anything about the rodeo. Her stomach knotted and she lectured herself for not talking to him about this sooner.

Adam left her side and took the stack from Bridget. "Thanks. Hey, did you finish up on the Baker's truck? They're wanting to pick it up this afternoon."

She nodded.

Their conversation faded in Faye's ears which were now buzzing while her heart hammered. Adam wanted to compete in the rodeo. Maybe it wasn't going to be so bad. Maybe he wanted to pick an event that wouldn't be terribly difficult. Hopefully, the process to compete wasn't going to be easy and he'd just forget the whole thing.

Adam wandered back to her, his gaze locked on the mailer in his hands. When he glanced up at her, he froze. "What?"

"When were you going to tell me you wanted to compete?"

"I did."

"No, you didn't."

"Yes," he drawled. "On our first date, I told you I wanted to do it. It's one of those bucket list things for me. Some people want to write a book. Others want to go skydiving. I want to compete in the rodeo."

"Then write a book."

His brows creased and he tossed the stack of mail on a nearby table. "What's gotten into you? This isn't news. I've been talking about it since we met. In fact, you've been teaching me how to handle a horse for this exact purpose."

"Yeah, but I always thought that you'd lose interest or realize that you don't have to impress a girl by risking your life."

Adam chuckled. "Getting on the back of a horse isn't risking my life. Do you—"

"Oh, yes. It is," she cut him off. "Do you know how many people die from horse-related accidents in real life?"

The humor fled from his expression. "No, but I feel like you're going to tell me real fast."

She tried to ignore the way his tight voice made her feel like she was doing something wrong. There was this tiny voice in her head telling her to drop this. Drop it now before it became a fight and she lost what she was so happy to have.

That tiny voice was right. This—whatever it was—was too new. She couldn't become the crazy lady who too quickly stomped out his dreams. Where would that put her? If he had gone after Dahlia, he would have had a support system.

Faye swallowed hard. She could do this. Taking a deep, measured breath, she let it out slowly and then nodded. "You're right. Of course, you're right. I wasn't thinking."

He gave her a funny look, closing the distance between them. His eyes delved into her as if they could read her soul, and it took every ounce of her strength to break that contact. He reached for her hand, rubbing the back of it with his calloused thumb. "Hey, what's going on?"

She shook her head. "Nothing. I'm fine."

"I didn't ask if you were fine. I asked you to tell me what this is all about."

She tugged her hand free of his grasp. Standing on her toes, she pressed a quick kiss to his cheek. "Sorry, I have to meet Eloise for a lunch date."

"But you said we could—"

"Sorry. I just remembered. I don't want her to think I bailed on her. I'll call you, okay?" She turned, walking backward before she blew him a kiss. "See you tonight?"

"Yeah," he murmured.

Faye hated seeing him looking so confused because she could also see the hurt behind his expression. She didn't know if it was due to her outburst about the rodeo or that she ended up bailing on him. One thing was for certain. She needed to get her head on straight, so when she saw him again, he wouldn't be able to corner her and demand that she tell him what it was all about.

Any excuse was better than the truth. How would she explain that him doing the rodeo terrified her? She could lose him just like she'd lost her mother. And then there was the issue of not discussing what they were to each other. How would he take that? Combine the two issues, and now this easy thing they'd found had become ten times more difficult.

20

Adam

It wasn't lost on Adam that his relationship with Faye was a little... strange. His previous relationships had been a little different than what he had now. First of all, every girl he'd dated before wanted to define what was going on between them. They wanted to know if they were exclusive or if they were allowed to see other men.

He'd grown to expect that sort of thing, and that was fine.

Faye was different.

Not once had she asked him where he stood on their relationship. The only time they discussed it had been right before their first date.

Both of them had agreed that they didn't like playing the waiting game, and that was about it.

Something was off about this relationship, but he couldn't figure out what it was.

Now there was something different brewing. Faye had

never really shown any adverse reactions to him wanting to do something in the rodeo. All her terse judgment had been reserved for Dahlia way back when they'd first started working on her mother's truck. What was different about it now?

Adam shrugged off the thoughts as soon as they appeared. He wasn't about to go messing up a good thing. He cared about Faye deeply. There wasn't a reason on earth for him to sabotage his relationship with her.

Besides, she'd been the one to take back what she'd said. How often had he done something similar? He could give her the benefit of the doubt. Faye was probably just having an off day.

It was funny how something as normal as pulling onto the Callahan property was enough to send his stomach into turmoil. It was probably due to the fact that he hadn't really had a good sit-down with Faye's father, and whenever he told people he was dating a Callahan, he got some pretty strange looks.

He'd heard the rumors. Zeke Callahan was a tough man whose only pride rested in his family and his family's ranch.

The thing was, Adam didn't understand how the man could have such a record with the town's folk, but Adam had yet to see any evidence for himself. After a few months of being on the man's property, both as a friend and as someone who was seeing Zeke's daughter, Adam hadn't bumped into the guy yet.

He pulled the keys from the ignition and climbed out of the truck. Usually, Faye was on the porch and they'd take off on a ride or a walk. This time she wasn't anywhere to be found.

Adam headed toward the house, glancing toward the barn as he did so in case she materialized over there. Maybe their strange conversation affected her differently. She had said to come by at five-thirty. He was only a minute early.

He knocked on the door but only got one rap out before it swung inward. Adam jumped back with a yelp. His eyes trailed upward and landed on the very stern features of none other than Zeke Callahan.

The man's eyes were the hardest Adam had ever seen. How had he gone his whole life and not crossed paths with Mr. Callahan in town? Adam cleared his throat and took another step backward that he hoped Zeke wouldn't notice. "I'm here for Faye."

Zeke grunted, his gaze sweeping over Adam much like he assumed a predator sizes up his prey. "You're just in time for dinner." He turned toward the house.

"Dinner? No. I'm here just to go for a ride or..." Zeke was already gone, the door left open. Faye hadn't mentioned dinner. But maybe this was the step forward she was offering him.

Adam crossed the threshold then paused. Why did he get the distinct feeling that this was a trap? The storm door slammed shut behind him and he jumped again.

The house was quiet and he wasn't quite sure which way to go—until a figure materialized around a corner.

Relief flooded his insides when Faye hurried toward him. "I'm so sorry. My dad sprang this on me like thirty minutes ago. I couldn't just tell him no—"

He grasped her hands in his. "It's fine. A little bit of a surprise—but fine."

Her brows were knit together, worry making the lines a

little deeper. "Are you sure? This is so new. We haven't really discussed meeting our families—"

"Faye, it's *fine*." He grazed her cheek with his thumb and offered her a reassuring smile. "I've been thinking we needed to do something about this anyway. It's about time we met each other's family officially, don't you think?"

Something flickered across her face, and she turned her head toward where he assumed the kitchen would be. "I should probably tell you—"

"Faye! You coming back?"

Adam tightened his hand around hers and tugged her forward. "I'm not scared of your family. Let's get some dinner, and then we can take that ride you promised me."

She mumbled something under her breath that he didn't quite catch. He probably should have asked her about it, but it wasn't important. Not right now. Based on what he'd heard of Zeke, he shouldn't keep the man waiting.

Voices rose the closer they got to the kitchen. When he arrived in the doorway, he paused. He knew Faye had a big family. But based on what he was witnessing, he wouldn't have classified it as large by any stretch of the imagination. Rather, the term was an understatement. Zeke stood at the head of an enormous table. There were six women and four other men seated before him like subjects of his kingdom.

Faye's hand tightened around his and she murmured, "I said I was sorry, right?"

Out of habit, he brought her hand to his lips and kissed it. "It's just your family."

"It's never just anything with my family," she muttered.

They headed toward the open seats at the table. Most of those already seated watched their approach. Adam let out a chuckle for lack of anything else he could say. "Sorry I'm late."

His focus flitted to Zeke, finding no trace of amusement in the man's expression.

He clamped his mouth shut, pulled out Faye's chair and then took his own seat. Did they have family dinners often? Or was this a special occasion?

A glance in Faye's direction didn't give him any clues whatsoever. She hadn't mentioned meals like this before.

Zeke cleared his throat and set his hardened gaze on everyone in the room. "Ever since I loosened the rules for you girls, I feel a distance has grown between us. You all spread out like dandelion seeds in the wind and didn't look back."

"*Dad*," one of Faye's sisters reached for Zeke's hand, "you know that's not how it is. We're all busy." Her eyes swept through the room. "But that doesn't mean we won't come home whenever you need us to."

Zeke's expression softened. "I know, Adeline. But with half of you married or dating," he said, his gaze zeroed in on Adam. "I felt the need to make sure we know what comes first." He let his words sink in before he continued. "That's family."

Faye's sisters exchanged smiles. The men in the room didn't seem the least bit anxious, unlike Adam, who now felt like this meeting was all because he hadn't come to meet Faye's father first.

He'd have to make sure to pull Zeke aside and apologize. That was the expected thing to do.

Right?

Zeke pulled out his chair and took a seat. "I'd like to have family dinners once a month. I'll not have any one of you become like strangers who no longer come around."

Chills rocked through Adam's body. Zeke might be intimidating, but he clearly was a good man. His own family was spread thin throughout the country. He himself had once been one of the seeds that had floated away. Adam glanced to Faye, who was giving her undivided attention to her father, and all he could think about was that he wanted her to have exactly what Zeke had described.

More than that, he might even want to be the one to stand by her side. The realization hit him like a bus. When he'd come back to Copper Creek, it had been with one goal in mind. He was going to take over the auto shop so his father wouldn't just hand over the reins to a stranger.

Bridget was great, and he enjoyed working with her, but he grew up in the shop. He wasn't about to let it go.

Then he'd set his sights on Dahlia—or maybe it was just having someone to spend his time with. He'd thought she would be a good option from the first moment he'd met her. She was beautiful, outgoing, and grounded. She'd grown up in Copper Creek, too. There wasn't a risk of her wanting to pick up and move, which gave him a sense of security.

And that was when he got to know Faye.

His gaze locked onto her. She was everything that Dahlia was and more. Plus, she had strong family ties. She loved horses and learning new things. She'd make a good mother.

A lump formed in Adam's throat. Up until this point, he hadn't really thought too far into the future. Not with Dahlia, nor with Faye. In the back of his mind, sure. He wanted a family—to settle down. But he'd never looked at either of these women as the way to get what he wanted.

Sitting at this table surrounded by Faye's family... he just knew.

This was where he wanted to be.

Faye must have felt his gaze on her because she turned toward him. He offered a smile—one she didn't return as readily as he'd hoped. Something was off. And he was going to figure it out.

Suddenly he didn't feel hungry. He didn't think he could stomach any of the food that smelled so good—not if Faye was struggling with something that involved him.

Adam itched to tug on her hand and pull her out of the kitchen so they could talk things over and get to the root of the problem. But he couldn't—not when he could feel the gaze of others on him. He was the new one—the stranger. He hadn't earned his place.

Not yet.

"So, Adam, you're the one who has been fixing up our trucks lately." It was the woman seated beside Zeke. She scooped some potatoes out of a bowl then passed it to the man seated beside her.

He nodded. "That's right, ma'am. I am."

Her gaze bounced from him to Faye. "I've seen you out here a lot on the weekends. Learning some tricks of the trade?"

Adam glanced at Faye with a smile. "I thought I might try my hand at the rodeo." He'd thought the room was quiet before. But that was when everyone had their silverware clanking against their dishes.

Now, this was quiet. He could have heard a pin drop on a pillow by the way the room went still.

Faye's sister appeared to be frozen, but it only lasted a moment. "Oh? Why is that?"

He swallowed hard. "Well, because that's what a lot of folks do out here."

The man beside her chuckled. "Wrong answer," he muttered under his breath.

Zeke shot the young man a sharp look then turned to Adam. "Folks out here work the land. We raise cattle and animals. We don't have time to showboat." His gaze flitted to Faye then back to Adam. "There is a time and a place for the events hosted at the rodeo. It brings in money for the town and some ranchers hire cowboys for that purpose. But not me. I won't risk the lives of my men in the arena."

Adam could feel Faye squirm beside him. This was where those comments had come from. She had been okay with teaching him the ropes when they weren't involved. But now they were. He couldn't help but feel that it was a little backward. Not once had she mentioned she was against him competing—at least not in the beginning.

Zeke pointed his fork at Adam. "You have a fine career, son. Don't squander the gifts the good Lord has given you."

He let out a strained chuckle. "With all due respect, sir. I've read the Bible. It also says not to hide your light under a bushel. We ought to explore our talents. Every single one of them."

Faye stared at him with wide eyes as if he'd told everyone he'd planned on joining the circus to become a lion tamer. When he glanced around the table again, he found everyone else had similar expressions.

Except for Zeke.

The man was as stone-like as a gargoyle.

The temptation to hunch down in his chair and disappear was one of the strongest he'd felt in a long time. He hadn't felt this judged since he'd moved out to the city after being raised as a country boy.

No one voiced their agreement which probably meant they were either too scared to do so or they simply didn't. Zeke didn't say a word. He simply reached for his glass of water and took a deep sip of it.

The conversation shifted as Grace brought up Riley's work with the equine therapy services. Adam didn't even know that was a thing. Apparently, everyone in this room was in favor of using horses in any way other than in the arena.

His frustration turned into embarrassment for once again not fitting in with the crowd around him. Then his embarrassment edged into bitterness. He'd been set up. Faye should have told him about these feelings a long time ago. She'd had so much time to do so; why hadn't she said something?

He kept his eyes trained on his plate the whole excruciating meal.

It took everything in him not to just get up and leave. He had to remind himself that Faye wasn't the type of person to sandbag him like this. She probably had a reasonable explanation.

Adam prayed she had one. Otherwise, she was proving to be just like others he'd met in the city. So many people who were only interested in serving themselves rather than the ones they should have cared about most.

21

———

Faye

Faye's horse plodded beside Adam's as they made their way along the trail. She should have known something was up when everyone showed up for dinner. She just didn't think that her father was going to attack Adam that way.

She should have never told her father that Adam was considering the rodeo. Trusting her father with stuff related to relationships wasn't a smart thing. Faye had seen first-hand how her father could get into the heads of her sisters.

The strange thing was that a part of her rationalized that Adam needed to hear every single thing they'd told him tonight. He needed a reality check, and he wasn't willing to get that from her.

Faye glanced at him out of the corner of her eye then let out a sigh. He was still visibly upset. Did that mean that he was going to follow her father's advice? Hopefully, he would see the logic in what her family had said.

The longer they rode, the more restless she became. She'd never been one to just let things fester. Taking in a deep breath, she prayed she could express herself in a way that he'd understand. Faye blew her breath through her pursed lips and faced him. "Hey."

His gaze cut to hers but didn't linger.

"I'm sorry about dinner."

"Yeah, you should be."

She blinked. That wasn't where she thought this would start. "Excuse me?"

"You totally threw me under the bus."

"I—what?"

Adam shifted in the saddle and faced her. "Yeah. You didn't tell me about dinner, and then when I showed up, I was thrown into this big family event without warning."

"I didn't—"

"And to make it worse, you let your family totally rip apart my dream."

She held up a hand. "Wait just a minute. First of all, I told you my dad sprang this on me thirty minutes before you got there."

"*Thirty* minutes? You couldn't have sent me a message? *Called* me?"

"I did." She hadn't had time to tell him this when he'd arrived, but now was as good a time as ever.

His mouth snapped shut.

"Yeah. I called the shop."

"The shop." Disbelief laced his words. "You called the shop when you could have called my cell phone."

"I got your voicemail when I tried your phone. I figured you were busy and I called the shop, but you didn't pick up there, either. I wanted to make sure you were okay with it, but since you didn't answer, I figured it was too late."

He shook his head. His dry chuckle didn't do much to put her at ease. "Fine. You have an excuse about dinner, but what do you have to say for yourself about what was said? Your dad made a fool of me. Everyone ganged up on me. You could have said something to put a stop to that."

"What do you want me to say? I told you that I didn't approve of the rodeo."

He threw his hands into the air. "Right. I forgot that you managed to neglect to tell me that little tidbit of information over the last several weeks of spending time together. I find it highly coincidental that you didn't have this opinion until after we started dating."

She scowled, turning her attention back to the trail. "If you had paid attention, you wouldn't be saying that."

"Oh? Please tell me when you alluded to the fact that you didn't like the rodeo. I'm all ears."

"I told you that you shouldn't participate in the rodeo to impress a girl."

"Yeah. I remember that. In fact, I recall it like it was yesterday. You told me that if I need to get bucked off a horse to impress a girl, then she's not the right one for me."

"See?"

He snorted. "Do you seriously not hear it? You told me that the girl wasn't right. Not the action."

"They're the same thing," She muttered in exasperation. "Putting yourself in danger isn't worth it. Not for Dahlia and especially not for a bucket list. You should be willing to walk away from stuff like that for a person. Be brave enough to say no." Her voice was strained and her heart pounded erratically. Just thinking about him doing something dangerous like that terrified her.

Adam didn't respond. Out of the corner of her eye, she could see him sitting stiffly. She wasn't about to believe that she'd gotten through to him. Adam was just as stubborn as she was, if not more so. He'd proven that in his determination to learn to ride.

She gnawed on the inside of her cheek and gripped the reins harder. "I lost my mother, Adam. I know what it's like to not be able to see someone I love for the rest of my life." This time she gazed at him, tears stinging her eyes. "I don't want to lose you, too."

The hard lines in his face softened, as did his eyes.

"I love you," she whispered.

There. It was out. She'd held these cards close to her chest for the last few weeks, unable to bring herself to admit her feelings to him or anyone else for that matter. She'd considered telling him a handful of times, but when she'd been tempted, her fear got the better of her.

Faye's lashes fluttered and she brushed at her eyes, attempting to conceal the fact that she was crying. Her emotions were too high. She was too close to the situation. This was the only hand she had left to play. "Please tell me you won't do it. Keep riding. Keep learning how to handle a horse. But don't throw away what we have because you have a fleeting interest in something."

"It's not a fleeting interest, Faye. At first it was to impress Dahlia. But after I got on that horse... I don't know. Something changed. I can't explain it. It's like the rodeo is calling to me."

"That's the most ridiculous thing I have ever heard." Faye hated the sharp way her voice spit out that statement. She grimaced and forced herself to take a deep breath. "What if I said I wanted to drive a car in a race like in those movies where they drift."

He snorted, but when he glanced at her, his expression sobered. "You couldn't do that."

"Why not?"

"Faye, that's completely different. First of all, you'd be handling a piece of equipment. Those cars are at least seventeen-hundred pounds."

"And bulls weigh approximately the same. Not only that, but they'll charge you. A car isn't going to chase me down once I fail at what I'm trying to do." Her argument didn't hold water and she knew it. But it was the only thing that Adam might relate to.

"Maybe not, but a car going fast enough will wrap around a tree and trap you inside. At least the rider can run from the animal."

"For heaven's sake, Adam. This isn't about the car. It's about the fact that you're willing to throw your safety away because you... what? You want people to recognize that you are a cowboy? You ride horses. You're learning how to lasso. For all intents and purposes, you're becoming a cowboy."

"It's not that," he muttered.

"Then what is it? Please help me understand," she begged. "If you can come up with a reasonable explanation, then I'll support you. But right now, it just sounds like you want to do it because you think it would be fun."

"That should be enough."

"But it's not. Too many people would be heartbroken to lose you. Your family. Your job." Her voice cracked. "Me." It wasn't lost on her that he hadn't returned the sentiment she'd shared earlier. Maybe he didn't care about her enough to make this promise. She pressed her lips together firmly. "I need you to promise me you won't do the rodeo... or I think we need to break up."

He'd been staring at his hands, fingering the reins as she'd given her little speech. But when she said those words, his head snapped up. Surprise was the only emotion that she recognized on his face. Was it a sign of progress that he wasn't angry?

Faye lifted her chin and set her firm gaze on him. "I will not put my heart in jeopardy. If you feel this is something you have to do, then you make that decision." Yes, she was aware that she'd just told him she'd support his decision if he had a good reason. But it was clear he didn't. He wasn't fighting for this, which led her to believe that he wasn't willing to risk it all —a fact that gave her marginal relief.

Adam worked his jaw, turning his focus back to his hands. "Fine. You're right."

Her brows shot up. It couldn't be that easy. She'd expected a bigger fight—that or Adam would choose his "dream" over her. Faye's stomach twisted almost uncomfortably. She straightened in her seat, squirming under his gaze. "Really?"

"Really." He ran a hand down his face and heaved a sigh. "I'm not an idiot, Faye. I know when I have a good thing. If you don't want me to enter the rodeo, I won't." Disappointment laced his words and made the rock sink lower in the pit of her stomach. He pulled his focus from her then motioned toward the trail. "Let's just forget this ever happened and continue our ride." Adam nudged Bella forward.

He hadn't told her he loved her in so many words, but he'd shown her he had feelings for her. Adam had been willing to give up something that he'd wanted to appease her.

She should be thrilled—over the moon, in fact.

So why did she feel so sick to her stomach?

〜

It had been a couple days since she'd seen Adam. Their last conversation hadn't exactly been a fight, so she didn't know why she was avoiding him. Everything had worked out. She'd gotten what she wanted, and he was okay with it. Well, maybe not *okay*. There were disappointments in life they dealt with every single day, and he was doing just that.

Faye stuck to her routine, riding her horses and finding work to do around the ranch. She didn't head into town as much, and the distance between herself and Adam continued to weigh on her.

She needed to get out of this funk she'd put herself in, but she couldn't figure out a way to do that. Faye thought back to their first real date. Adam was a romantic. If she could bring herself to stop by the shop, maybe she could surprise him with something. Or maybe she should ask him out on a date?

Faye groaned, and her father eyed her from where he sat at the head of the table. She chewed on the inside of her cheek and fiddled with the fork that had been placed near her plate. There was no way she was going to ask her dad for advice after the meal they had shared with everyone. He was part to blame for what happened.

Then again, she should probably thank him, too. He'd managed to get everything out in the open and force her to confront Adam about the rodeo issue.

Nope. She wasn't going to talk to her dad about this. She was going to figure it out on her own.

Faye pushed away from the table and picked up her plate. It was early, but Adam would likely be up. She could call him, or she could just show up at the shop and surprise him with coffee.

Her heart fluttered. That was the first sign that she was on the right track. She *did* love him. She wanted this to work out. Avoiding him wouldn't allow that to happen.

"You going somewhere?"

Faye froze, her back to her father. "I was thinking of going into town."

"To see that boyfriend of yours?"

She sighed. "Yes, to see Adam."

"Is he still planning on joining the rodeo?"

Facing him, she placed one hand on her hip. "I should have never told you that. But if you must know, he said he wouldn't sign up."

Her father grunted, nodded, and turned back to his newspaper.

"You know, you didn't have to attack him at dinner... in front of everyone."

Zeke didn't look up at her. He kept his eyes trained on the paper in front of him. "I didn't attack him."

"Okay," she drawled. "You didn't have to embarrass him. You put him on the spot."

He peeked at her. "Life is full of uncomfortable situations. We are a close family. If he's even remotely serious about dating you, it's better for him to be fully aware of what that would entail sooner rather than later."

"We only recently started dating. That doesn't mean we're going to get *married*."

"That boy has been coming around for months. Don't pretend this only began a few weeks ago. Trust me. Adam plans to stick around."

She didn't know if his words thrilled her or terrified her more. Perhaps it was a mixture of both. Adam hadn't said he loved her even after she'd said it first. She'd thought he would have said those three words before leaving that night, but she refused to push the issue. He needed to *want* to say it.

Even still, she let her smile spread from ear to ear. "You really think so?"

Her father glanced up at her once more, a brow lifted. "I know so." He folded his newspaper and placed it on the table before getting to his feet. "Do you know if Brielle is home?"

She shook her head.

"Well, if you see her, tell her I'd like to speak to her."

"Is something wrong?"

His left cheek twitched and his jaw tightened. Taking a deep breath, he set his firm gaze on her. "You all think I'm unaware of what goes on beneath my roof."

Faye stared at him blankly.

He leaned closer to her. "Let me tell you something. This is my domain. I know what is happening at any given moment, and I'm tired of looking the other way. I'm done pretending, and Brielle needs to stop skulking in the shadows. It's time for her to grow up and take responsibility for her life."

She gaped at her father. Was he suggesting that he knew about Brielle's unsavory escapades? She'd been the first one to break their father's rules. She'd been the one who continued with those habits even after the rules were lifted.

And their father had known.

Faye could feel the heat start in her stomach and spread outward. Her face flushed and she avoided meeting his gaze.

"You'll tell her I want to speak to her?"

She nodded. "If I see her, I'll let her know."

He placed his hand on her shoulder. "Thanks."

22

Adam

Adam pulled the socket wrench around one more time firmly then reached out to check the bolt. It wasn't going anywhere, and now the car he'd been working on all week was done. All he had to do was reset the diagnostic and contact his customer.

Then it would be on to the next car and the next one after that. The daily grind had really become what everyone had said it would. There was nothing new or exciting about his job. He had recently lost the vibrance his life once held. It was as if Zeke Callahan had sucked the enthusiasm Adam once had for life right out of him.

That wasn't fair.

He couldn't blame Zeke for all his own misgivings lately.

Adam could only blame himself.

Faye had made several valid points. He'd even looked up the stats. While deaths weren't the most common, several riders ended up with head trauma or other serious injuries every year from rodeo accidents. Some of those said accidents would incapacitate him to the degree that he wouldn't be able to do his mechanic work. He had managed to pick one of the most dangerous hobbies there was.

And yet, it still called to him. There was something missing in his life, and he hated that he couldn't put his finger on it.

Once upon a time, he'd felt the same thing and ended up leaving this place for a life in the city. But that life had ended much in the same way.

Adam had returned to Copper Creek.

He'd told Faye it was to run his family's business—that he knew he belonged here. But the more he thought about it, the more he realized it wasn't true. He had loved being back for the first little while. But then things inevitably turned stale.

What was wrong with him that he couldn't be satisfied with everything he'd been given? He had a girl he cared for. He had a job and a future here. So why did he still itch to find something?

Adam tossed the wrench into a toolbox and grabbed the oil rag from his shoulder. The door to the shop slammed open, and Bridget froze there. They both did.

"You forget something?" He shoved the rag in his back pocket and stared at her expectantly.

At first, she didn't move. Then she tossed some envelopes on a nearby bench and strode toward him. "Um... no. Do you even know what time it is? It's six in the morning. Were you here all night?"

He glanced toward the dark windows at the top of the garage doors. They were dark much like they'd been a few hours ago when she'd left. "Nah, that can't be right. You're pulling my leg."

She shook her head, concern creasing her brows. "It's six in the morning, Adam." Her shrewd eyes shifted toward the car he'd just finished. "That was an eight-hour solo job, at least. Don't tell me you're done with it?"

Adam didn't bother answering the question. "Fine, I lost track of time. Is that what you want to hear? I'm sorry."

"Don't apologize to me. You can't charge extra. You know that, right?"

"I wasn't going to do that," he muttered as he brushed past her. "I'm just a little distracted."

She followed him through the doors and into the main area of the shop. "Distracted about what? Maybe I could help."

"I doubt it." He collapsed into the office chair behind the reception desk and leaned his head back. His eyes closed, and he couldn't deny how the exhaustion seemed to wrap around him. A curse slipped between his lips and he pinched the bridge of his nose. He wasn't going to be any good to anyone today at the rate he'd been going.

"Don't tell me this has to do with your girlfriend."

Adam's eyes flew open and he stared at her. "It doesn't." That was a bald-faced lie, and he knew better than to try to hide things from Bridget. She was a savant with that sort of thing. The way she cocked her head and shot him a pointed look was enough for him to know she didn't believe him. "Fine. Yeah, we sorta had a fight. But it wasn't really a fight." He dragged his hand down his face, heaving a sigh. "I don't know what it was. But I don't like it."

"Clearly." Sarcasm. Great. Bridget had no sympathy for him. She was probably going to tell him to get his butt out of this chair, go home, get some rest, and then deal with Faye like he should have in the first place.

Only he didn't know exactly what that meant. Was he

supposed to tell her she was wrong and go for what his heart wanted? Or was he supposed to suppress those feelings and accept that the rodeo stuff just wasn't in his cards?

"Adam."

His eyes sought out hers, and he forced himself to maintain eye contact. "What?"

"I can tell something is up. We all can. You're distracted, working odd hours, and you're not even doing your best work. Whatever it is, you need to get a handle on it."

Adam bit back the instinct to reprimand her for talking to him that way. She wasn't his boss. She didn't even have any ownership in this place at all—though he had been considering giving her an opportunity to become a partner of sorts. She was always the first to arrive and the last to leave—besides himself of course. If anyone deserved to get some perks out of this place, it was her.

Instead of biting her head off, he leaned back in his seat. "I'm doing just fine. I have a few things to hammer out and then I'll be back to my old self." At least he hoped he would. This whole rodeo thing had turned him upside down and inside out.

"Well, until you get it all sorted, I'm going to get to work. And maybe you should go home and get some rest."

He rolled his eyes. "I'm fine."

"No, you're not. You can't operate heavy machinery in your state. What would your father say?"

Adam shook his head. "My father won't have to know about any of this as long as you don't tell him. The work is getting done. The customers are happy. Let's just leave it at that, shall we?"

Bridget threw her hands into the air then strode toward the shop. She didn't have to agree with the way he was handling things. She just had to accept it for what it was.

The door opened, and without looking up, he muttered, "We open at eight. Come back in two hours."

"I thought maybe you'd make an exception for me."

Adam sat up straighter in his seat and stared at Dahlia. He blinked, tempted to rub his eyes. He was hallucinating, right? Never had she come into his shop before. Their only interactions had been at the past rodeos and when they'd bumped into each other at the country club. Now she was here, and he couldn't help but feel something was off.

He got to his feet and leaned over the counter, offering her a tired smile. "What do you need? Is your car running okay?"

Dahlia glanced over her shoulder to the darkened parking lot. "I think I need an oil change. But I'm going out to the next town over and I have to be there around eight."

Before he could say anything, she held up both hands. "I know, I know. You don't even open until then. But I was driving by after picking up my usual coffee and saw the lights on. I figured it was worth a shot."

Adam twisted around to stare at the shop. Bridget wouldn't be thrilled to do an oil change this early when she likely came in to do stuff she actually enjoyed. It was beyond him why she preferred some of the more mechanical stuff when the shop was set up to make oil changes so easily. He rubbed the back of his neck and nodded.

"Sure. I think I could get you in. But it's going to cost a little extra."

She smiled as she placed the keys on the counter. "Sure, no problem."

He picked them up and took two steps toward the shop when she stopped him. "Did you hear about the rodeo?"

Adam's heart stuttered. He'd started to associate that word with feelings that weren't all that great. It was far too easy to recall that dinner he'd shared with Faye's family and the judgment he'd endured. "What about it?"

"They never come to Copper Creek. But they are this year. In a couple weeks, they'll be doing all the main events at that local arena."

He turned toward her. "Really?"

Her smile widened as she nodded on her way toward him. "Yeah. And this year they're doing something really cool. They have three events specifically for rookies. Anyone can participate, and the winners will win money."

The anticipation got him. He didn't know where it came from or why it felt like it had hit him over the head with a two-by-four, but it was there. And then it disappeared. "Yeah, but I bet there's a cutoff to register." What was he thinking? He couldn't register. He'd promised Faye he'd stay away from the rodeo.

"That's the beautiful thing about this one. People can register right up until the event. They won't be cutting it off until ten minutes prior. I guess the organizers of this one has a soft spot for newbies."

Or they had a wicked sense of humor. If what the Callahans had said about the rodeo was true, then the majority of those who registered would likely get hurt. If he hadn't promised Faye already, he could be one of the guys who suffered.

Adam shook his head. "I don't think I can. Faye wouldn't—"

"Faye? Don't tell me your girlfriend makes all your decisions for you. That's not right."

He stared at her, once again unable to move. His brain was all muddled from the lack of sleep. Everything she was saying sounded right.

Dahlia took a few more steps toward him, closing the

distance between them. "You can't keep living your life for other people. You came here for your dad. Now you're staying away from your dream because of a girl? You want to know what I think?"

Adam couldn't bring himself to comment.

"I think that if she's going to be so bothered by it, just don't tell her. Faye sure doesn't seem like the kind of girl who would even attend the rodeo. If I had to bet, I'd say you could register, participate, and have a story to tell when it's all done. If she can't see that this would make you happy, then she needs to let you go."

Was Dahlia seriously telling him that he should break up over this? Faye hadn't asked too much of him. She'd only asked him not to compete. If he couldn't abide by her wishes, wasn't that a sign they weren't going to be good together?

A small, sinister voice reminded him that they probably were already past that. He'd been so quick to consider breaking his promise that it would take very little to actually complete the deed.

His eyes focused on Dahlia once more. "You really think she wouldn't find out?"

Dahlia shook her head. "I really don't." She dug through a large tote that was draped over her shoulder and pulled out two sheets of paper. "The top one is the flyer with all the information about the rookie events. The bottom one is the one you'd mail out. Take a quick look. You might even find you aren't interested. But if you are, you'll have one fan in the stands to cheer you on." She gave him a little wave and hurried toward the door. Stopping just before she pushed it open, she turned to face him. "When did you say my car will be done?"

Adam glanced at the old clock on the wall. "I'll have

Bridget bring it in right away. We can have it done within the next thirty minutes."

She beamed at him. "Great. I'll be back at seven to get it if that's okay. I'm just going to wander down the street and get me some coffee." Her eyes swept over him. "You look like you've been hit by a bus. You want me to bring you anything?"

He shook his head. "I'll be fine. We have a coffee maker in the back." Yeah, a coffee maker that made the world's worst coffee. He just didn't want to lead her on. Already she knew more than he'd wanted her to. She could tell his relationship was on the rocks. Well, that was all she was going to be privy to. He wasn't even sure he'd tell her if he signed up.

Adam picked up the papers she'd left with him. The cash prizes would be nice. Not only that, but the winners would get to attend the regional rodeos for free for the next year.

The door opened again, and without looking up, he murmured, "Forget something?"

"Hey."

His head snapped up and his heart dropped to his knees. Faye stood just inside, her hands behind her back. She was dressed from head to toe in a blue jumpsuit.

"Where did you get a ridiculous thing like that?" he asked with a smirk.

She glanced down at her clothing and let out a small laugh. "I might have accidentally borrowed it."

"Stolen it, you mean?"

Faye moved closer, and he scrambled to cover the pages he'd dropped with something else. He prayed she hadn't noticed his movements. If she saw those papers, their relation-ship was over.

She leaned her hip against the counter and jerked her head toward the shop door. "You need anyone to hold a rachet today? How about wipe windows? Put me to work and maybe we could go get lunch." Faye leaned over the counter, concern etching in her face as she placed her hand to his cheek. "Actually, you don't look so great. Do you want me to take you home? Are you coming down with something?"

Adam grasped her hand and pulled it away so he could kiss her palm. "I pulled an all-nighter. I'm just tired."

Her frown deepened. "Why did you do that? I thought the point of working here meant you were in charge."

He grimaced. "That *is* a perk, and actually one of the reasons I was able to get away with it."

"You didn't get away with anything," Bridget interjected.

Flinching, Adam ducked as if doing so would make him invisible.

Faye chuckled. "I think you got caught," she whispered.

"I think you're right."

Bridget stood there with her hand on her hip. "Faye, please take him home so he can at least get a few hours of shut eye. Bring him back after he's done that and gotten some food in his stomach."

"I'll go, but that means you have to do me a favor."

"Fine. Whatever it is, I'll do it if you'll just get out of my hair."

He tossed her the keys in his hand. "Change the oil in this? The customer needs it by seven because she's going to be doing a lot of driving today."

Bridget scowled at him, and for the first time in a while, he drew pleasure from it. "Fine. Now, leave," she muttered. "Don't you dare come back before noon."

"Yes, ma'am."

23

Faye

It was worse than she thought. Adam was clearly having a rough time of it, and she couldn't help but blame herself. Gone was the man who had an easy smile that could make her feel as light as a cloud.

She nibbled on her lower lip as they exited the building and headed out into the parking lot. "You want to get some breakfast?"

He glanced at her. "I'm not really hungry."

Faye didn't know why, but his statement made her heart splinter. It was early, and he hadn't slept all night. She shouldn't even be worrying about herself. This was about making him feel better. "How about I take you home and then pick you up for lunch?"

They stopped at his truck. He rested his wrist above the driver's side door and glanced up at the sky, which was starting to brighten. "Nah. I'm good. I'll head home and then we can meet for lunch. How does that sound?"

Once again, she felt like she was on the outside. Every option she came up with, every action, she couldn't see an outcome where he would welcome her back into what they once had.

"Hey." Adam's features pinched and he stepped away from the truck toward her. He traced his thumb along her jawline, causing chills to erupt along her arms. "What's the matter?"

Faye grasped his hand and held onto it, studying the lines there along with the callouses and the grease beneath his fingernails. "Are we okay?"

The first indication she got that they were anything but was that pause. The silence stretched between them far longer than she was comfortable with. When she lifted her gaze to meet his, she only caught a glimpse of something that confirmed her suspicions. Just as quickly, he schooled his features. He smiled as he slipped his hand behind her neck and pulled her in for a kiss.

His lips brushed against hers for the briefest of moments —too fast for her to really enjoy it. Then he released her. "Lunch," he promised. "We'll do lunch."

Faye nodded. "Okay."

Adam climbed into his truck and shut the door. She waved at him through the window before he started his truck and drove down the street.

Everything would be okay. He was just tired. That was all. Once he got some rest, he'd be back to his usual self.

"You feeling any better?" Faye leaned over the table at Sal's Diner and reached for Adam's hand. It looked like he'd showered and gotten a few hours of sleep. But he still didn't seem like himself.

He offered her a smile. "I'm doing better." If this was supposed to reassure her, it did the exact opposite.

She let out a sigh and settled back into her seat. "Can you tell me what's bothering you?"

Adam jumped as if she'd caught him off guard.

"I'm here for you. Whatever is bothering you, I can help you with."

His eyes flicked up to meet hers then dropped to the menu on the table in front of them. "I'm good. Promise."

She snorted, her frustration growing. "No, you're not."

"Yes, I am. It's just been a rough couple of days."

"You mean since that meal with my family."

The way his eyes locked onto hers, she knew that was it. There was a darkness that hadn't left since they'd walked away from the kitchen table. She was definitely to blame. Did he hate her family so much that he would rather sulk about a dinner gone wrong rather than flesh it out?

"Yeah, that's what I thought. You hate them, don't you?"

His brows lifted. "Hate them? That's a bit strong."

"Well, don't you? After dinner you were upset that I'd put you in an awkward position."

He huffed, a dry chuckle filling the air as he shook his head. "Awkward position. You think that's what this is about?"

"Isn't it? You weren't thrilled about being there with my family. I told you that they were a lot to handle, and you insisted that you could handle them. I knew we should have just taken off and skipped out."

Adam shook his head again. "And if we had done that, how would your father feel about me then? If he was so quick to judge me based on an interest I have, then he *definitely* wouldn't approve of me for skipping out on family dinner."

"He would have gotten over it," she insisted. "It was too soon, and that's partially my fault."

She had thought for a moment that he'd comment back, but all he did was let out a sigh and straighten in his seat.

The waitress arrived and they placed their orders, but as soon as she left, Faye turned back to Adam. "I—"

"Let's just have a nice meal together, okay?" Adam's weak smile did nothing to ease her conscience. "I've had a long couple of days and I'm just starting to feel normal." He traced his thumb over her knuckles. "I've missed you."

"It's only been a few days."

"Well, going from seeing you nearly every day to *not* seeing you made me suffer withdrawals." He cocked his head to the side, his eyes studying her.

Faye squirmed beneath his gaze, wishing she could read his thoughts. The words she had on repeat in her head since she'd stopped by his work finally forced their way through. "I'm sorry," she blurted.

"About what?"

"About not warning you about my dad. About not sticking up for you."

Adam's eyes narrowed. "Are you saying that you would be okay with me competing in the rodeo?"

"Oh, heaven's no. I've seen far too many accidents in the arena. It's not something I would ever want anyone I cared about doing."

He leaned closer, his brows furrowed. "You realize that no matter how much you try to protect someone, they're always going to be in danger of *something*. We're mortal. Kids fall off bikes and out of trees. People get in car accidents or plane crashes. What about football?"

"Yeah, but those activities aren't like the rodeo."

He pulled his hand from her grasp, dropping it into his

lap. "How can you say that? What if I wanted to do something at the rodeo that wasn't riding a bronc?"

"Do you?"

"Well, no, but—"

"Exactly. And it's not just your safety I'd be worried about. Those horses don't want riders. They'll fight hard when someone is in the saddle. But other horses don't care and they get prodded into bucking. The whole thing is just... ridiculous. I don't know what everyone likes about the whole thing anyway."

Adam reached for his rolled-up cutlery. He rubbed the napkin between his fingers. "I suppose we'll just have to agree to disagree."

That rock in the pit of her stomach weighed on her more than before. Was she making a mistake with her request? It was for his own good. He *had* to see that. They needed a change of subject. That's all.

If she could get him talking about something else, then they could get through this, and it would be in the rearview mirror.

"I heard that there's a meteor shower happening soon."

Adam glanced up at her, and she thought she saw a ghost of a smile. "Where did you hear that?"

She blushed. "I might have looked it up."

"*Might* have?"

Faye lifted a shoulder. It was the only thing she could think of to connect with him. Stars and cars. But saying that out loud probably wouldn't sound so great. She pressed her lips together before grinning at him. "I just wanted to do something fun with you. Get back to what we were before—" Faye snapped her mouth shut and the flush returned to her face. "I just want to spend time with my boyfriend. So, what do you say? Should we get some stuff put together and head out to where we can see it? Maybe take a picnic?"

"Sure, that sounds fun."

Their food arrived. Adam got a cheesesteak sandwich with au jus and dove right in. Faye picked at her burger, still feeling like there was a distance between them that hadn't been remedied. "Would it be okay if I hang around the shop with you?"

His eyes cut to meet hers. "Don't you have stuff to do back home?"

She shook her head. "I told my dad I wouldn't be around today. Today is all about you. I can be like your assistant. I've got almost all the tools memorized, and I can get you water or coffee. Whatever you want."

Adam seemed to consider her for a moment before he nodded. "Sure, why not?"

~

"CAN you get me that socket wrench? Make sure it has the three-eighths ratchet on it."

Faye jerked into motion, hurrying to get what Adam had requested. Bridget had already given them more than her fair share of strange looks, and Faye had just about had enough of it. She held out the wrench and leaned on the edge of the car. "So, what are you doing with this one?"

"Just a tune-up. Changing fluids and checking a few things," Adam muttered without looking at her.

"So pretty easy?"

He took a deep breath and exhaled, which only made her feel like she was doing something wrong. She probably was. She'd practically pushed herself on him today.

But in her defense, she really wanted to fix this rift. Brielle would probably tell her she was trying too hard and that she needed to wait for Adam to come to her. But the problem they were having wasn't his fault. It was Faye's, and she wasn't about to shy away from fixing something she broke.

She pressed her lips together in a thin line then turned around and leaned against the car while surveying the room. Nothing much had changed about this place. It was still the same old mechanic's shop she'd been in when they'd fixed up her truck.

Bridget was working on a truck on the other side of the garage, and the only sound besides the faint country music playing was that of metal clanging against metal. Bridget straightened, stood back and admired her work, then glanced in Faye's direction.

Faye stiffened when Bridget headed in their direction.

"This one's done." Bridget stood nearby.

Adam poked his head out of the hood of the car. "Good. Put together the paperwork and we'll give them a call."

"What about that oil change this morning?"

He hit his head on the hood of the car then withdrew, rubbing his scalp. "What about it?"

"Dahlia seemed to think you weren't charging her the full price."

Faye froze.

Dahlia.

The Dahlia.

The woman who Adam had a crush on had been here. Faye swallowed back the unease that crept up her throat. Bridget had said she needed an oil change. The woman wasn't here to steal Adam away; she just came to the only mechanic in town.

Adam sighed. "What did you charge her?"

Bridget placed her hand on her hip. "I charged her the usual rate. I'm not letting her get away with something."

He rolled his eyes. "I told her there'd be a surcharge for coming in before we opened."

A slow smile spread across Bridget's face. "I guess it's a good thing I added a little extra to the bill." She winked at Faye. "You know, because she's a little much." Bridget sauntered off then called over her shoulder, "If you think it was too much, you can offer her a credit or something. She paid it in full, though, so maybe just leave it be."

Faye spun to face Adam. "You didn't tell me that Dahlia came in."

He ducked in under the hood again. "Why would I need to tell you that?"

"Because..." Faye bit back what she was about to say. Jealousy didn't look good on her, and that was the last thing she needed to add to the mix.

Adam withdrew and gave her an expectant look. "Because?"

She crossed her arms. "Because I thought we told each other everything."

Something strange flickered across his features. He dove back under the hood and got to work. "She needed an oil change before heading out to a few rodeo events that are nearby. I told her I'd go ahead and let Bridget handle it."

"The rodeo is back?"

"Yeah," he grunted.

Tension filled the air between them. This was a sore subject, and Faye knew better than to believe it would go away so soon.

"Adam?"

"Hmm."

"I want you to know how much I appreciate you."

He grunted.

"Thank you so much for staying out of the rodeo. I know you were interested, and maybe in the future—"

"I signed up, Faye."

She choked on her words, her stomach knotting and her lungs refusing to bring in the oxygen she needed. "What?"

Adam pulled away from the car and rubbed his hands on an oil-soaked rag. "I signed up for the rodeo. I'm not getting any younger, and after having thought about it for the last couple of days, I knew I needed to."

"You *needed* to," she muttered in disbelief. "You *promised*," she accused. "You said you'd stay away from it. I don't understand. Why would you do this to me?"

He shook his head, and she couldn't understand why he was so calm. Meanwhile, her heart pounded like it was about to explode. He was going to get on one of those broncs and get seriously hurt or worse.

"You can't."

Adam lifted a brow. "I can do what I want to do with my life. You can make your choices too. If this is something that is a deal breaker, then..."

"Then what, Adam. Then we break up? Well, it sure seems like you don't care about me nearly as much as I care about you." She let out a heavy groan and paced beside the car. "I'm not asking you to cut off a limb here. I'm just asking you to think clearly about this."

"I *am* thinking clearly. I'm not going to let you pressure me into not doing this. I'm going to do what I want to do for a change."

She whirled around and faced him, a snort escaping her lips. "You have *always* done what you want. You left here when you didn't want to be a small-town boy. You came back when the city wasn't working out for you. And now you're joining the rodeo like it's the next big thing. You're not thinking about this at all." She threw her hands into the air. "I can't do this. I *tried*. I even confessed my feelings for you. And what do you do? You break the promise you made."

Faye stormed toward the door.

"Where are you going?" he called after her.

"Home. Call me when you grow up."

24

———

Adam

Adam stared at the door long after it slammed shut. All day long, from the moment he handed over his signup form to this very second, he'd thought about what might happen when he finally told Faye.

In his defense, he'd felt cornered into making that promise. He hadn't been given the chance to really think it over. He'd been interested in competing for a few months now. How could Faye ask him to just let go of that interest when their relationship was so new?

That was the cause of his foul mood. *That* was the reason he couldn't focus or sleep lately. And the fact that all it took was one conversation with Dahlia for him to go back on that promise was enough to make him realize he wasn't ready to give up on his dream.

He should feel guilty. That would be the normal response. He probably should apologize to her. Knowing Faye, she was feeling betrayed by what he'd done. A spark of that guilt he'd been expecting ignited, but he snuffed it out. No one had the right to tell him what he could or couldn't do in his free time. If he wanted to try a new hobby, Faye nor anyone else could stop him.

"What did you *do*?"

Adam swiveled his focus to Bridget, who stood beside the door leading to the waiting area. She had her hands on her hips and her face contorted with suspicion.

"*Please* tell me you didn't do anything stupid."

He shrugged.

"Oh no, you don't." She stormed toward him. "Faye has been acting like a puppy dog around you all afternoon, and suddenly she charges out of this place like you slapped her across the face. What did you do?"

His defenses went sky-high. "Why do you assume that I'm the one who did something? What if she's the one who did something? Have you ever thought about that? A few days ago, I went over to her house and she had a family dinner."

Bridget set him with a dumbfounded look. When he didn't elaborate, she threw her hands in the air. "Oh, heaven forbid your girlfriend wants to introduce you to the rest of her family. You can't seriously be angry at her for that."

"It wasn't the dinner that was the problem. It was that her family tore me apart." He crossed his arms as if the act alone would keep the woman in front of him at bay. This was why they didn't have women mechanics in the city. Too many hormones. Up until this point, Bridget had stayed out of his love life—well, for the most part. It was like she didn't care until Faye got hurt.

If Faye was upset, it was by her own hand.

Bridget still stared at him with expectations, and he groaned. "You know I wanted to compete in the rodeo."

"Yeah? So?"

"Well, apparently the Callahans are against the rodeo. They don't compete, and they don't support competitors."

She snorted. "I doubt that."

"You'd think I was making this all up, but I'm not. Zeke considers the rodeo a necessary evil. It brings in money, but it's dangerous and he won't let his ranch hands participate either."

"Well, he's smart."

His head reared back. "Aren't you married to a cowboy? Aren't your cousins cowboys?"

Bridget pursed her lips to the side and her eyes narrowed. "Yeah. So believe me when I say this. Zeke is a cautious man. He lost his wife at a young age, had to raise his daughters on his own. Everyone in town knows what he's been through, and no one is going to second-guess his decisions when it comes to keeping those he cares about safe. If he doesn't want you to compete, it's because you mean something to him or his family."

Adam's jaw slackened. He hadn't thought about it that way. From what he'd experienced, he was being targeted because he was different or new in the family.

None of that mattered at this point. Faye didn't want anything to do with him, but he wasn't about to walk away from this. It wasn't like he was going to leave his job at the shop to be a rodeo cowboy. Why couldn't anyone understand that he deserved to accomplish some of his goals?

He scowled at her. "That may be, but it doesn't mean he's right. I can choose to do what I want. I deserve to be happy, too."

"Let me ask you this. Did Faye make you happy?"

"Of course."

"Then you're an idiot." She spun on her heel and headed back the way she came.

"What?" he called after her.

"You heard me."

He charged after her. "Yeah, I did, and I can't believe that you're actually blaming me for this."

She whirled around to face him, her eyes flashing. "From what I heard, you don't care about Faye or her family. You don't care about the people in your life. You care about *you*. You only want to do what makes you happy, and that's it. You know what I call *that*? Selfish."

Her words left a sour taste in his mouth. He wasn't being selfish. Didn't people say all the time that it was best to take care of oneself before they had to take care of others? His happiness was important. How could he help others be happy if his cup was drained?

When he focused on her again, she'd made it through the door and into the waiting area. His hands balled into fists and he strode back to the car he'd been working on.

Bridget was only saying this stuff because she'd found her true love. He cared about Faye, but did he love her? He thought he did, but then this whole debacle happened, and now he didn't know.

Adam paced back and forth beside the car. Everything that Bridget had said echoed right along with everything Faye said. It was getting harder and harder for him to be able to ratio-nalize what he'd done.

Perhaps he should have told Faye this morning where he intended on going. Then at least, she would have been able to let the information settle while he slept.

He stopped and raked a hand through his hair. Well, it was too late now. He wasn't going to withdraw. He needed to know what it was like to be in that arena—to see if he was capable of hanging with the cowboys. It was like he needed to prove not only to himself but to everyone else that he belonged in Copper Creek. He wasn't just a mechanic. He was so much more than that.

"You're looking good out there."

Adam pulled on the reins of the horse he'd borrowed from Shane and turned around in the corral. The rodeo was in a few weeks, and he needed to get more comfortable on horses he wasn't familiar with. It was all about confidence at this point. But at this moment, he wasn't getting that confidence, mostly because his audience was none other than the woman who'd triggered this decision in the first place.

Dahlia rested her chin on her folded arms that rested on the corral bar. Her makeup was done perfectly, and she wore a cowboy hat that shaded her face just right to show off that bright red lipstick she wore. Her head tilted slightly, and she offered him a bright smile. "I didn't know if you'd follow through with it or not, but I'm glad you did." She glanced around the immediate area. "What does Faye think about it?"

He cleared his throat and pulled his gaze away from the woman. Being within even a few yards of her made him uncomfortable for some reason. Perhaps it was the way he'd avoided telling Faye about her visit. Or maybe it was because he still harbored feelings for Faye, and he was in denial that their relationship was over. "She's not too thrilled about it."

Dahlia pouted. "That's what I heard. I'm sorry. You deserve so much better than her."

If she'd heard about their little fight, there was no way she didn't know that he was no longer dating Faye. But he wasn't about to point that out. He needed to focus. He'd risked everything he thought he'd cared about for this, and he was bound and determined to prove Faye and her family wrong.

He tugged on the reins to pull the horse around and toward the middle of the corral. Focus. Confidence. If he could handle speed, he could handle staying on the horse, right? He'd watched several videos online to see tips and tricks. The more he watched, the harder it became to maintain that self-assurance.

"When is the competition?" Dahlia called after him.

If only he could pretend that he couldn't hear her, then maybe she'd leave him be. Adam glanced over toward her to find her now inside the corral and leaning against the bars behind her. She offered him a flirtatious smile.

He heaved a sigh, urging his horse into a faster gait. "In a few weeks," he hollered at her.

"I can't wait," she said.

He thought that was the end of the conversation, but then she climbed up on the fence and crossed her leg over her knee provocatively. Her skirt barely came to her mid-thigh, and if he looked hard enough, he might have seen more than he was prepared to.

There would be no staying focused. Having Dahlia here, uninvited, was too big of a distraction.

His eyes narrowed and he put his weight on his toes, pushing his horse faster.

Dahlia whistled—loud.

The horse threw his head and reared up. It was only one jump, but Adam hadn't expected it. He held tight to the reins with one hand and the saddle horn with the other, but it didn't stop him from falling from the back of the horse just like he had in front of Faye. A cloud of dirt exploded up around him as his backside landed in the dirt. The horse trotted to the far side of the corral. Adam lifted his head to watch him go and then dropped his head back to the ground.

A groan seeped from his chest after he caught his breath.

"Oh, my gosh! Are you okay?" Dahlia ran over to him, kneeling at his side. Her hand trailed over his arm. "I'm sorry, I didn't realize your horse would do that. I thought it would be better trained."

"Me neither," he bit out.

"Well, you should probably figure out how to stay on better if you want to stand a chance in your division."

He shot her a sharp look. "You realize I wasn't trying to ride a bronc, right? I was getting some practice in riding and momentum."

She let out a giggle. "Yeah, but didn't you say you wanted to do bronc riding? That horse didn't even kick up his legs."

Adam waved her off as he dragged himself into a seated position. She scrambled to her feet, reaching for his hand to help him up, but again he waved her off. He glanced at her once before he swiped up his hat from the ground and dusted it off. "I appreciate your support, but I think I'll be able to focus a little better if I work on my own for the rest of my practice session."

She stepped toward him and her lower lip puckered. "Oh, are you trying to get rid of me?" Her finger traced little circles on his chest. "We used to spend a lot of time chatting as we watched some of the competitors. I thought we were friends."

He grasped her finger and tugged it away. "We are friends. That's why I was willing to change your oil before the shop even opened. But right now, I need to focus, and I need quiet."

Dahlia tilted her head in what she probably thought was a flirtatious motion. "Well, maybe you could make it up to me and meet me out at Sal's for a piece of pie when you're done."

"I'll let you know." He brushed past her. That was weird. It wasn't until recently that Dahlia had shown even a smidge of interest in him. Now she seemed to be showing up at every turn.

He glanced over his shoulder to find her slipping through the corral bars and heading toward the club. This could be a sign. He'd wanted to date her before. It wasn't until he spent more time with Faye that he had dropped his interest in Dahlia. Maybe this was how it was always supposed to be.

Adam shrugged off that thought. If he even entertained that possibility, wouldn't that just be him going on the rebound? Dahlia deserved better than that.

Faye deserved better than that.

All at once, his heart lurched, shattering and crumbling. He clutched at his chest and focused on taking a deep breath. If it weren't for the fact that only his heart was hurting, he might have thought he was having a heart attack. The moment passed, and he shrugged off the unease that swarmed him.

He grabbed the saddle horn and shoved his foot into the stirrup before climbing into the saddle. The only way he was going to get over Faye was to continue staying focused on the plan. He'd get through the competition. Then he'd see what his heart wanted. It was entirely possible he wasn't meant to be with anyone at all.

Adam dug his heels into the horse's flanks and moved him forward. Around and around the corral, faster and faster. If only he could go fast enough to escape from the pain, longing, and guilt he currently felt.

As much as he tried to push Faye from his thoughts, he was unsuccessful. The lump in his throat grew and his breathing shortened. His head pounded, and he had to pull the horse to a stop before something bad actually happened.

Who was he kidding? Practice was over for the day.

25

Faye

Faye gripped the steering wheel of her mother's truck as her stomach roiled. Everywhere she looked, everything she did, she couldn't stop seeing Adam's face. His smile and his laugh haunted her. It had only been two weeks since she'd last seen him, and they had been the worst weeks of her life. Her head and her heart continued to battle over whether she'd been too harsh on him. She ended up rationalizing that Adam had lied to her by omission and that deserved the reaction she'd given him.

This wasn't just about the rodeo anymore. This was about him losing her trust. He wanted something badly enough that he'd gone behind her back to do it. If that wasn't a sign, she didn't know what was.

Her face heated and a tear escaped her eyes as she pulled onto her family's property. If this was the right decision, then why did it hurt so much?

It got harder to breathe when she felt this way. Adam had been the first guy she'd ever confessed her feelings for. He'd been the one that she had entertained spending the rest of her life with.

And yes, she knew that fantasy was ridiculous. People couldn't just fall in love with the first person they met. And if they did, it was better for them to date around before settling. Divorce rates being what they were, Faye was smarter than to believe she'd get her happily ever after with someone who had such different views than her own.

That logic only infuriated her more. Falling in love was supposed to be easy. Hadn't her sisters all found their soul mates? Was there something wrong with *her*?

Faye heaved a sigh and pushed the door open before climbing out of her truck. She slammed the door shut a little harder than she probably should have and stomped toward the house. Her mood left much to be desired, evidenced by the way anyone crossing her path on the property gave her a wide berth.

Flinging open the door, Faye marched inside and headed for the kitchen. If she was lucky, everyone would have already eaten dinner by now and she'd just be able to have the food that was left over. Usually, someone fixed a plate for her and put it in the fridge.

She slowed as she got closer to the kitchen, voices giving her pause.

"Someone needs to talk to her. She's scaring off the hunters."

"She's fine. Just leave her alone and let her figure things out. This was her first crush. She's allowed to be heartbroken."

Faye burst into the kitchen, glaring at her sisters, Sean and her father. The other men in her sisters' lives weren't at the table, which was probably for the best with the way she was feeling. "Adam wasn't just some *crush*." She breathed heavily even though she hadn't been exerting any energy. "I *loved* him. I could see us getting married and spending the rest of our lives together. That's how deeply I cared for him. Everything was great until that dinner we had. Everyone made him feel like an idiot. That's when the problems started. So if you want to talk to me about my attitude, maybe you should all look at yourselves and figure out what you did to contribute to the failure of my relationship." She spun on her heel and stormed from the room, her appetite lost.

Her skin was flushed and her hands shook with the fury that was quickly blinding her. She charged up the stairs to her room and slammed the door for good measure. Once inside, she let her gaze sweep over the room and that's when the exhaustion claimed her.

Faye stumbled backward and leaned against the door. She slid down the wood, her hands over her face and let out a sob.

This wasn't how it was supposed to go, and it wasn't just the breakup. She was supposed to be an empowered woman who could look at this situation with clarity. What happened to her that she couldn't get over this ache that had spread from her heart to the rest of her body?

"Faye?"

She stiffened, her sob catching in her throat. There was no distinguishing which sister was behind her door at that moment. It could have been any one of them. Whoever it was sure had the nerve to come up to her room right now.

The doorknob rattled and the door bumped against Faye's back. "Faye, it's Brielle."

"And Eloise."

Faye rolled her eyes. The only two sisters who weren't married or in relationships. They wouldn't understand what she was going through. "I don't want to talk to either of you," Faye shot back. "Just leave me alone."

"You know we can't do that."

"Yeah. If we go back down there, they're going to ask us how it went."

They murmured something to each other that Faye couldn't hear, then Brielle's voice came down low right behind Faye's head. "Just let us in. You can tell us what happened."

"You *know* what happened." Faye leaned her head against the door with a thud. "He wants to do the rodeo, and I wasn't comfortable with it."

"That can't be the whole story."

The anguish Faye felt only expanded and another fat tear rolled down her cheek. No, that wasn't the whole story. But right now, no one could grasp what she was dealing with. Faye got to her feet and pulled the door open. "I don't know what to do."

Brielle and Eloise moved in on her, pulling her into a tight hug. No words were uttered, and they didn't need to be. Their compassion was felt fully in that moment.

Faye moved to her bed and sat on the edge. "I feel like an idiot." She didn't bother looking up at either one of her sisters. They wouldn't understand anyway. It was just nice to have someone to talk to who wasn't going to tell her what to do.

"What happened?" Eloise sat beside her and draped her arm around Faye's shoulders. "Because I can tell you one thing. You're not an idiot."

Faye snorted. "Wait until you hear what happened." This time she glanced up to meet first Brielle's gaze and then Eloise's. "You remember that dinner when Adam said he wanted to be in the rodeo? We went on a walk, and he promised me he wouldn't sign up."

Neither one of her sisters said a thing, but based on the

way Brielle's single brow lifted, she didn't approve of something. Or maybe she didn't believe that Adam would do something like making a promise like that.

Clasping her hands together, Faye took a deep breath and let it out. "He seemed a little out of sorts for a few days, so I went over to make him feel better." She nibbled on her lower lip then let out another heavy breath. "He told me he signed up anyway. He broke his promise, so I ended it. And now I don't know if I did the right thing." She shook her head firmly. "No. I did the right thing. I just didn't think it would hurt this much."

"You did the right thing," Eloise murmured as she rested her head on Faye's shoulder. "If Adam is going to go against what he said, that's not a good sign." She glanced up at Brielle. "Right? Faye doesn't want to be with someone who won't stick with what they said."

"True..." Brielle drawled. "But..."

Faye snapped her gaze over to her sister. "But what?"

Brielle lifted a shoulder. "You can't really blame him, can you? I mean, you guys haven't been dating for very long. He promised something when he was under duress."

"He wasn't under duress," Faye spit out. "He promised to make me happy."

"If you say so."

Faye shot to her feet. "What are you not saying? He didn't *have* to make that promise."

"Well, when he made that promise, it was right after everyone told him it was a bad idea, right?"

"Yeah, so?"

"When you went on the walk, who brought it up first?"

"He—" Faye cut herself off. "I don't remember."

"Well, if it was you, then you only further pushed him to do something he wasn't comfortable with. What if the tables were turned? What if he pushed you to do something you didn't want to do?"

Slowly, Faye settled back on the bed. "I don't know."

Eloise patted her on the back. "It's fine, Faye. You have to go with your gut on this one. If breaking up with him felt right—"

"That's just it, though. It doesn't feel right." She set sad eyes on Eloise. "I miss him. More than that, I knew he had an interest in the rodeo when we met. I just didn't realize how deep it was. Is his interest in the rodeo really something worth breaking up over?"

Brielle crossed her arms. "We can't answer that for you. But if you want my opinion?"

Faye nodded.

"I've lost someone before. The ache never goes away." Her eyes were more serious than Faye had ever seen before. "*Never*, Faye. Yes, you'll move on. You'll fall in love again. It's like grief. You'll carry that weight with you every single day of your life. People we fall in love with take a piece of us. It doesn't matter how long you loved them. They will still hold a part of you."

Chills coursed through Faye's body. She wasn't sure if it was due to her own crumbling heart or the knowledge that Brielle was struggling with something similar, and she'd not even noticed.

Her thoughts shifted to what her father had said about Brielle's escapades. Was he aware of the broken heart Brielle was nursing?

"Besides," Brielle continued, "cowboys are like wild horses. They can't be tamed. They're not meant to be controlled. We can break them to a degree, but their heart is always going to go where it wants to go the most. If that's you? He'll be back. Just do yourself a favor and don't make him choose."

Eloise snickered. "Adam is hardly a cowboy, Brielle. Have you seen him ride? I saw him get bucked right off his horse one day. I hope he isn't trying out for something that requires him to stay in the saddle." The humor on her face faded when Faye shot her a dark look. "Oh. Well… then I bet he'll be fine. He's probably been practicing." She got to her feet. "How about I get you something to eat? I'll be right back."

The second Eloise was out of the room, Brielle settled beside Faye. She didn't say anything right away, causing the air between them to grow more uncomfortable by the second. "You can ask me if you want, you know."

"Ask you what?" Faye glanced at Brielle out of the corner of her eye. She wasn't going to assume a thing when it came to Brielle. She was the sister that all of them didn't quite understand. She'd gone against the grain at every turn.

"About the guys."

Her head whipped around, and she stared at Brielle. "*Guys*? You've fallen in love more than once?"

Brielle laughed. "*Ouch*."

Faye grimaced. "Sorry. I just didn't realize that you—"

"Be careful with what you say next," Brielle cautioned.

Clearing her throat, Faye looked away. "Who did you fall in love with?"

"You can't say a single word."

"I won't." This must have been really juicy information if Brielle was making Faye promise to keep quiet. Her whole body tingled with anticipation.

"Back in high school, James and I had a thing."

"*James*. As in James *Pratt*. Constance's *James*?"

Brielle dug her elbow into Faye's side. "Shh! Yeah. We had a thing, and once upon a time I thought we'd end up together." She gave Faye a wistful look. "Of course, I don't have the same feelings for him that I used to, but I will always wonder what would have happened if I hadn't pushed him away."

"Brielle, I had no—"

"Then, for a while there, I had thought Shane might be the guy who would pull me out of my slump."

Faye blinked several times. "I knew you went on a few dates with Shane, but..."

Brielle gave her a sharp look. "I don't want to hear a single word breathed about him. That was a breakup that I needed for personal reasons, but like I said. He made his mark. My point is, you can fall in love several times and it might not be the right guy. Just..." She let out a sigh. "Just do what will make you happiest. If that means going for the guy who has some questionable hobbies, then do it. There are worse guys."

"Like Wade Keagan?"

Brielle slapped her knees and got to her feet. "Well, I'm done. Nice chat."

Faye straightened, laughing. "What? Wait, I'm sorry."

"Nope. Just... nope." There was a smile on Brielle's face, indicating she wasn't upset. But it was definitely a touchy subject. Faye settled back on her bed. Everything Brielle had said made sense—enough that she knew she'd have to sleep on it before making a final decision.

26

───────

Adam

dam turned his cowboy hat around in his hands as he watched the current competitors do their stuff in the large arena. The cowboys riding the horses would get their steeds to run fast and then come to a skidding halt.

At the speed those horses were running, it was impressive to see them sliding for upwards of ten feet. He couldn't tell why such an event was important enough to put in the rodeo, but it was nice to watch—especially if it got his mind off his own event.

His gaze swept through the arena, taking in all of those who came for the rodeo. There were people of all kinds in cowboy hats and boots. Men and women and children eating greasy food, watching the rodeo events, and playing the carnival-like games.

For the first several hours, Adam had searched for a specific group of people. He'd hoped to see even one person from Faye's family though he couldn't really figure out why. That family had flat-out told him he was wrong for wanting to do this.

If pressed, he would have to admit to himself that he wanted to see Faye more than anyone else. He wanted to hear her laughter, to have her cheer him on. He'd envisioned being here differently. He'd always thought she would be by his side when he finally ended up in the saddle.

Adam frowned as he put his hat on his head and strode away from the arena. He wove in and out of groups of people, not sure where he was planning to go. He'd already paid for the entrance fee. To walk away would be a mistake.

Unless being here was the mistake.

Faye knew this world better than he did. In all likelihood she was right about the dangers that the rodeo presented. And maybe he was just being stubborn. Didn't he deserve to be happy? Wasn't that the whole point of living? He should be able to try new things even if they were dangerous. That was what made people feel alive—the thrill of it all. And really, was the rodeo as dangerous as Faye had made it out to be? He'd been here all weekend and hadn't seen one instance where someone needed to leave in an ambulance.

Adam continued to wander along the paths that had been carved out by the guests attending the rodeo. Food vendors and craft tables had been set up, and on the other side of the property, cowboy music played. He hadn't been in that direction, but he'd heard there were live performances, and it wasn't just a DJ.

Happy couples and happy families moved like the waves of the ocean. They followed the currents of the people in front of them. Children ran ahead of their nervous parents only to be reprimanded a moment later.

He eyed a family with a young girl and boy just ahead of

him. Each parent held a child's hand as they made their way toward the area where carnival games had been set up. The little girl skipped beside her father, pigtails floating with each step. She wore a small pink cowboy hat with matching boots.

For some reason he couldn't understand, his thoughts shifted to what it would be like to have his own child—to have someone so dependent on him. Right now, the only one that would really suffer if they lost him was his father. His brothers would be sad, but they'd get through it.

And Faye.

Except she'd broken up with him. She didn't want anything to do with him. How much could she actually love him if she was willing to throw away their relationship, as new as it was, over something like this?

A pair of cowboys and a small boy made eye contact with him, going the other direction. One smiled wide and stopped. "Adam, right?" He was familiar, but Adam couldn't place him.

Brows creasing, Adam nodded. "Yeah."

"I thought it was you." The man turned to the other cowboy. "This is Faye's boyfriend. He's the guy I was telling you about." He turned to Adam again. "Looks like you ended up at the rodeo after all." He nudged the guy beside him. "After that dinner you missed, I didn't think he'd have the guts to do it." He chuckled. "Zeke can be one hard cookie, right?"

Adam glanced from the man with the boy to the man in front of him. The guy was familiar, but he couldn't recall seeing him at that dinner. "I'm sorry, I forgot your name."

The man chuckled again, extending his hand. "Riley. I had you fix up my motorcycle a ways back. I'm Grace's fiancé."

Memories came flooding back and Adam smiled broadly. "Right. You were the one who helped Faye pay for her truck's parts."

"That'd be me." Riley gestured toward the other cowboy.

"This is Tristan and his boy Mathew. He's with a Callahan too." His focus swept over Adam then shifted as if searching the nearby crowds for someone. "So, what event are you competing in?"

"I've signed up for the bronc riding. It's in a few hours."

Riley grimaced. "I'm guessing that isn't going over very well with Faye."

"You could say that," Adam muttered.

"Where is she?"

Adam rubbed the back of his neck. Either he hadn't heard that they'd broken up, or he was pretending he didn't. Either way, he was putting Adam on the spot. "She's not here."

Riley and Tristan exchanged glances then Riley gave Adam a short nod. "That's tough. I'm sure she'll come around, though. The Callahans are stubborn, but they're pretty smart."

Mathew tugged on Tristan's hand, drawing his attention. He pulled until his father dropped down and then whispered something to him.

Tristan straightened. "I'm going to take Mathew to the bounce houses. It was nice to meet you, Adam. Good luck." He made a face. "You're going to need it."

They watched Tristan leave then Riley nudged Adam. "Don't listen to him. He's got a lot on his plate. When you have someone to care for, you tend to be... well, there's no nice way to say it... a nervous wreck. It took a lot to get him out of his shell, especially when it came to letting his boy ride. Faye will figure things out. You'll see."

"You're telling me I should do this then?"

Riley chuckled. "I think you should do what makes sense. Would I do it? That's a big no. I've seen action. I'm more than happy to keep my feet on the ground."

Adam studied Riley. What kind of action was he referring to? Had he been a rodeo competitor? He shoved aside his curiosity, pressing Riley for more information. "What would you have done—had you wanted to compete?"

Rubbing his chin, Riley seemed to consider Adam's question deeply before responding. "I suppose I wouldn't have pushed it. I love Grace too much to make something so small become an issue. I'm all for a man following what calls to him. It's just a matter of what's more important. In your case, there are probably a lot of other things you could do with your time. Let me ask you this. Do you see yourself turning this into a career?"

"No." There was zero question what this was. Like learning how to skydive or going rock climbing, the rodeo was something just for fun.

"Do you love Faye?"

That was a question he hadn't expected. He had feelings for her. There was no question about that. He hadn't admitted it out loud to anyone. Adam worked his jaw back and forth then nodded. "Yes. I do love her."

"Then I guess the only question you have left to answer is whether this ride is more important than making her happy. Relationships aren't fifty-fifty."

Adam's eyes narrowed. A relationship between two people would definitely add up to each taking half of the responsibility.

Riley chuckled and clapped him on the shoulder. "When you're in a relationship, you should always be giving one hundred percent—even if your partner isn't. There are going to be days when you can't fulfill your end and days when she can't either. You should make sure you're giving all of yourself whenever you are capable."

"What are you, a therapist or something?"

This time he tossed his head back and let out a loud laugh. "Sort of. Though, I never saw myself being one. Anyway, if you're beating yourself up over this, then maybe it's not the right decision. Perhaps you need to step outside yourself and figure out what you really want before you go through with it."

The man had to be a couples' counselor. There was no other explanation for the advice he was giving.

"And what if the damage has already been done? What if she doesn't want me back?"

Riley frowned, his head tilting only slightly. Okay, so he hadn't heard about the breakup. He considered Adam for so long that Adam began to twitch. Then he took in a deep breath and let it out. "I'm not going to say that there's always a way back. Faye is her own person. She's permitted her feelings, same as you. But I will say this much. You're never going to know unless you try." He glanced at his watch then offered Adam a smile. "Sorry, but I have to get going. Tristan and I are headed to an auction. Good luck with everything. Like Tristan said, you're gonna need it."

Adam watched him go, letting his advice settle. A lot of what the man said tracked. What was the rodeo, but one more thing he'd decided to chase when he felt his life was empty? But then he'd fallen for Faye. She'd fulfilled him in ways that nothing else had.

"Adam! It *is* you. I wasn't sure you were going to follow through." Dahlia glanced around. "Where's your girlfriend?"

He stiffened. "She's not here."

She frowned, moving closer to him. Her hand grasped his forearm. "That's a shame. Is everything okay between you two?" Her voice seemed to change, softening somehow. "Is she upset that you're here?"

Attempting to step back without drawing too much attention to himself, he nodded. "We're fine."

"Really? Because if everything was *fine,* she'd be here." She pouted. "You deserve better, Adam. A guy like you should have the support of a woman who loves you." She tilted her head as she trailed a finger up his chest. "I heard that she didn't even want you to sign up."

His brows furrowed. Either someone had overheard their fight at the shop, or Faye was spreading what had happened between them.

Dahlia leaned in closer, her whispered voice beside his ear giving him chills. "I wouldn't prevent you from doing something you want to do. *I* learned a long time ago that cowboys can't be controlled—they *shouldn't* be." She pulled back just far enough for him to meet her eyes. Her tongue trailed along her lower lip and her eyes dipped to his mouth. "What do you say? Are you free later?"

Adam froze. This was unexpected, to say the least. He'd thought he'd gotten to know Dahlia well enough before he asked for Faye's help, but since he'd started spending more time with her, Dahlia had become a stranger. She'd never been this forward before now.

The funny thing was that she was no longer alluring to him. He didn't see her the same way he saw Faye. He didn't want any of this.

At that very moment, she stood on her toes, framed his face with her hands and leaned in.

27

Faye

Faye didn't even know what she was doing here. Today was the busiest day for the rodeo, and the whole place was filled to the brim with people coming for everything from the livestock auction to the competitor events.

A couple collided with her, nearly knocking her over. Despite being out in the open, she felt claustrophobic. She should have just called him or left him a message. That would have been better than surprising him—here—at the rodeo.

Ahhg! She was being way too impulsive.

What did she expect would happen? It's not like she could just show up and tell him she wanted to work things out. That couldn't possibly go over well at all.

Faye nearly turned around, but something caught her attention.

Not something.

Someone.

Adam stood about ten yards away.

Seeing him brought back all the emotions she'd thought she had buried. All her misgivings fell away. She could do this. All she needed to tell him was that she'd overreacted. Their relationship was more important than their argument.

She took a step toward him, ready to call out his name, but then she stopped herself.

Dahlia stepped up to Adam. She touched him and leaned in closer to him.

Faye's stomach churned and her heart turned over. This couldn't be happening. They'd only been broken up for a couple of weeks. It hadn't taken him much time at all to move on. And with Dahlia, no less.

It was like watching a train wreck. She couldn't tear her eyes away from him. The way Dahlia moved closer made it clear she knew what she was doing. She was confident.

She rose on her toes, and that's when Faye had to turn around. Her breaths came out in rapid, short spurts, and she charged through the crowd. Emotion burned in the back of her throat. It felt like her heart was trying to claw its way up and out of her body.

Her stomach continued to toss. Faye needed to find a quiet place to get her bearings. She crossed her arms as she ducked behind a taco truck. Faye leaned against the trailer, letting it support her head. Shutting her eyes did nothing to block out what she'd just seen.

If anything proved that she had made a grave mistake, it was the way she felt right now in *this* moment. She didn't want to date anyone else—be with anyone else—but Adam.

She'd been feeling cruddy since their family dinner—like she'd been in limbo. Her heart knew what she wanted. The only thing that made her second-guess where she stood was those feelings of doubt.

So what if she hadn't dated as much as Brielle? Faye had taken a different path. She'd befriended Adam first. She'd gotten to know him and what made him tick. She knew how to make him laugh and what was important to him.

And that was the rodeo.

Why had she gotten in her own way? If the situation had been flipped, she wouldn't have been too thrilled about Adam demanding that she change.

Her eyes flew open, and she sucked in a breath as if she'd been starved for oxygen before she came to this realization.

She wouldn't make Adam pick between his dream and her. That was one mistake she'd never make again. But she wasn't about to let Dahlia swoop in and steal him away from her. That woman was one of the shallowest people Faye could think of. She'd only developed feelings for Adam because of his interest in riding. Faye didn't know how long Adam had flirted with Dahlia before she finally realized what she was missing, but she was too late to the game.

Dahlia didn't know Adam like Faye did. She wasn't in love with him.

Faye pushed away from the truck and lifted her chin. She wasn't going to give up without a fight. That wasn't in her blood. Adam needed to know how much she loved him and that she would wait for him for however long it took.

If that meant supporting him in a sport she despised, so be it. But she needed to confront him about his feelings for Dahlia first.

28

───────

Adam

Adam held up a hand, successfully stopping Dahlia from stealing the kiss she was intent on taking. Her eyes cut to his and she plopped back down on her feet. Crossing her arms, she gave him a confused, albeit hurt expression. "Don't you want me? You've been flirting with me since the day we met several months ago."

He took a step back. His focus swept through the immediate area as if looking for someone specific, but he knew better than to hope that Faye was here. This interaction with Dahlia had grown ten times more uncomfortable than he was ready for. Adam rubbed the back of his neck, bringing his gaze back to Dahlia. "I'm sorry."

"You're *sorry*?" Dahlia huffed. Her brows lowered, eyes flashing. "You're sorry. That's all you have to say about leading me on?"

Mouth falling open, Adam took another step back. "I wasn't leading you on. I was just—"

"Yes, you were. You flirted with me. Then you asked me to dance. *Then* you fixed my car. What else am I supposed to believe?" She put all her weight on one foot and threw her hands into the air. "See? This is why I don't date guys like you. You're all the same. You say whatever it takes to get on a girl's good side, and then you gaslight her."

"I—what? No. I wasn't doing that." His mind was racked with confusion. He hadn't done any of that. Well, he'd flirted with her before he'd met Faye. But neither of them had acted on that flirtation. Was he missing something?

He searched within himself. The only thought that crossed his mind in the moment that Dahlia had nearly kissed him was Faye. He didn't want Dahlia's affection whatsoever. He'd fallen hard for the cowgirl who could rein in a horse with little effort. He wanted the woman who knew what she wanted—moving heaven and earth to get it. He wanted Faye because of her passion for life.

Adam set Dahlia with a firm stare. "I'm sorry, Dahlia, but I'm not interested in going on a date with you. I've got a girlfriend."

"Really? Because a true girlfriend would be here right now, supporting her man. She wouldn't let a good one slip through the cracks."

He smirked at her. "Well, it appears you made the same mistake."

Confusion briefly filtered across her face, but he didn't have any time to revel in it. He needed to get this conversation over with so he could call Faye and apologize for breaking his promise. If she'd still have him, he was willing to mend the bridges they'd burned.

"If you wanted to date me so badly, then why were you

only interested in me when I told you I was training to be in the rodeo?"

Her jaw dropped, then her cheeks filled with color.

"From the looks of it, you have a type, and it has nothing to do with a man's character. I'd rather be with someone who wants me for me and not for the things I enjoy doing. Ironic, isn't it? You were only interested when I wanted to be part of this whole show, and Faye just wanted to keep me safe."

Dahlia snorted. "Good luck winning her back. I heard about your little breakup. You *lied* to her. How much you wanna bet she throws you to the curb? I'll give you a tip. Girls don't like liars."

"Then why are *you* asking me out?" He forced himself to ignore the fact that someone had eavesdropped while they had their argument at the shop. He'd have to be more careful about what he said and who he said it to.

She shifted her weight from one foot to the other and her coloring deepened. "Well, you didn't lie to me."

He snorted. "You think guys like me are all the same? How about you look in the mirror. You might be surprised at what you find. There's a lot you could learn about what guys want in a woman." Adam shook his head, brushing past her as he dug into his back pocket for his phone.

Time to stop making mistakes and excuses. Women like Faye were few and far between. He'd met people like Dahlia in the city. That was one reason why he'd left. It sure looked like he wouldn't be able to escape people like Dahlia wherever he went.

All the more reason to make things right with Faye.

He lifted his phone to his ear and plugged his other one. The phone rang until it went to voicemail. She was avoiding his calls. Of course she was. What did he expect?

He might actually have to leave the rodeo to get her to talk to him.

Adam heaved a sigh and glanced at the time. The bronc riding wouldn't start for another hour. He wouldn't have time to leave and come back, but at this point, he was willing to forfeit. Doing so might blacklist him, but that was a risk he was willing to take.

"How could you!"

He knew that voice. The harmonious tone easily wrapped around him like the memory of his childhood blanket despite being laced with fury. Adam turned around and a wide smile spread across his face. "You don't know how glad I am to see you."

"Really? Because it sure looked like you were more than happy with the company you shared about twenty minutes ago." Faye stormed toward him and poked him hard enough in his chest to force him to take a step backward. "How could you?" she repeated softer this time. He could practically taste the agony in that question. The look on her face tore him up inside.

"How could I, what?"

"Don't play dumb, Adam. I saw her. I know you were here with Dahlia. Just…" She shook her head and her shoulders drooped. "Don't lie to me anymore. I can't take it."

Without considering what he might do or say to make this better, he reached out and grasped her hands with his. "No more lies. I swear it." He gave her another smile, then reached up to tuck a strand of hair from her face before capturing her hands once more. "I was talking to Dahlia, but I'm not here with her. She cornered me."

Faye looked up at him, her eyes shining with what he could only assume was hope. Had she come here to hash things out? His heart flipped and he suddenly felt lighter. If

Faye was here to talk, then he might have a chance after all. He'd have to tread carefully, but if he did this right, he might end up leaving with the most exciting girl this side of the Colorado River.

Adam held her hands firmly, as if doing so would prevent her from walking out of his life a second time, but he knew better than to believe he could stop her. Faye had a mind of her own, and he wasn't going to stand in her way.

He cleared his throat.

Here goes nothing.

29

Faye

Fury, pain, and desperation whirled tumultuously within Faye as she waited for Adam to explain himself. She'd learned her lesson. She wasn't going to fly off the handle and tell him she wasn't interested anymore.

The truth had been proven more than once.

She wanted to be with Adam. She wanted to share her love with him and no one else.

Her fears of the unknown would have to take a backseat to that, no matter how hard that would be.

Adam released her hands and moved his own to grasp her upper arms. He rubbed them up and down. "I'm not going to lie to you. Never again, Faye. I shouldn't have signed up without telling you."

The wind left her sails as she stared at him. His voice and eyes had softened to resemble the man she'd fallen in love with. Gone was the moody individual who had been lost to her.

He let out a heavy sigh and shook his head. "Combining two lives will never be easy. I'm positive that we won't see eye-to-eye on everything. But we'll have all the time in the world to do that. I just know I want to spend that time with you."

Faye didn't know what it was about his words that softened all the hard edges of her heart. But at this point she didn't have to explain it. She let out a shuddering breath and forced a smile. "That's really sweet of you, but..."

"But?" The edge returned to his voice, and even though they were surrounded by several people coming and going, it felt like they were alone together.

"But you don't have to change who you are to be with me."

The spot between his brows creased, and his grasp on her tightened slightly.

Faye couldn't bring herself to maintain eye contact with him. She'd been the one in the wrong. That much was clear. She'd overreacted. She'd broken up without a thought as to why he did what he had. And worse, she manipulated him into making a promise he wouldn't be able to keep.

Her cheeks burned with the embarrassment. "I don't understand why you want to stay with me so much."

"Because—"

She held up a hand and stepped back. "I need you to hear me out."

Adam nodded.

"I should have never forced you to promise me anything. Our relationship being what it was—it wasn't fair to you. In fact, it wasn't fair to either of us. I set you up for failure."

He shook his head. "That's not—"

"Please let me finish." She stared at a spot on his chest, right above his heart, drawing all the courage she needed to say what had to be said. "I'm new at this relationship thing. I didn't have a chance to make all these mistakes with relationships that wouldn't matter down the road. For that, I'm sorry." She forced herself to meet his gaze. "I ended up making all the mistakes with the person I loved, and I realize I shouldn't have treated you that way."

The next part was going to be the hardest thing she would have to do so far, and she thought apologizing for her behavior was mortifying.

Music from the intercoms died down and an announcer's voice blasted through them instead. "Bronc riders, make your way to Arena A."

Adam stiffened. Every part of him, from his face to the muscles in his arms, hardened. "I'm not—I don't have to go."

Faye tilted her head, lifting her hand to his cheek. "I'm not going to stand in your way, Adam. I'm here to support you in whatever capacity it is that you need."

For a brief moment, which actually felt more like an eternity, he stared at her. His gaze penetrated her right through to her soul. It was almost as if he was worried that she was trying to trap him.

She reached for his hand, lacing her fingers within his, then brought his hand to her lips. "I mean it. I want you to be happy. You are more than just the guy who fixed my mom's truck. You're more than the guy who can make me laugh. You're just... so much more than I deserve." Her voice broke and she had to tear her focus from him or risk bawling like a baby.

He hooked his finger beneath her chin, tilting her face up gently to look at him. Chills raced through her body, pinging against every raw nerve she had.

"I love you," he said.

Her lashes fluttered in an attempt to keep the tears at bay.

Up until this point, she wasn't even sure he had the same degree of feelings for her that she shared with him. He'd kept that sort of confession to himself.

Adam cupped her cheek within his palm, and she leaned into his touch. His thumb traced over her cheekbone and his eyes roved over her face. "I think I've loved you since that moment you came into my shop and asked me to help you fix your mother's car. It was clear from that first moment that your heart isn't like all of the other hearts I've interacted with in my life. You care far deeper and with more sincerity than anyone I know."

Her breath shuddered as she exhaled. "I love you too, Adam." She couldn't bring her voice above a whisper and wasn't even sure if he'd heard her.

It was as if they were locked in a reality where it was just the two of them. Their connection with each other was stronger than it had been before. In this moment, she knew that she'd made the right decision. Whatever they had to go up against, they could do it together.

"Final call for Bronc Riding contestants."

He glanced up, away from her face, and their trance was broken. The sounds and smells of their surroundings returned, nearly knocking her off balance. Adam pulled her in for a hug, crushing her against his chest. "I don't have to go."

She craned her face around and stared at him with a seriousness she hadn't had in a while. "Yes, you do. Something about this event is calling to you."

Adam shook his head. "It's true that I've been searching for something my entire life—trying to feel like I belong somewhere. I'm happy, then I get to a point where I feel like something is missing." He gave her a pointed look. "I don't feel that way anymore."

30

———

Adam

dam's heart sang. There was a part of him that knew he had finally figured it out. Faye had been missing from his life. He hadn't realized it until Dahlia had tried to kiss him. He wasn't going to be happy with just anyone. And he was too smart to believe that dating someone would solve his problems. Faye was the one he wanted to be with because she loved him.

And he loved her.

There was something special about their bond that he would likely never understand.

Faye tightened her arms around him before standing back. "You can't be certain about that."

He frowned. "What do you mean?"

"There's a reason why certain things call to us. It might be a person, or a truck, or the sky..." She grinned, then tucked a strand of hair behind her ear. "I know better than to fight a feeling like that. I think you should do it—if you want to."

Adam couldn't believe what he was hearing. She wasn't just telling him what she probably thought he wanted to hear. She was insisting that he follow through with what had come between them.

He felt a little off-balance. Wasn't it wrong for him to get everything he wanted when he'd made all those mistakes? It didn't seem fair.

She reached for his hand. "Besides, this is a small town. Do you really want the guys you fix trucks for to think you're too scared to get on the back of a horse?"

"But you hate this sort of thing. It's dangerous." He found himself making excuses, not because he didn't want to compete, but because he wanted to make sure she was certain of her decision.

Faye's smile faded but only slightly. "I want you to be happy more than anything. Men make a career out of this. You're just wanting to cross it off your bucket list, right?"

He grinned at her, tilting his head. "Well..."

Her mouth dropped open. There it was. That concern showing through. This was harder for her than she had let on.

Adam laughed. "Don't worry. I'm not the least bit interested in making a living from being thrown off horses that don't want me riding them. I think I'll stick to keeping my head under the hoods of the trucks that come into my shop."

Relief flooded her features, then she pushed him playfully. "Don't scare me like that."

They made it to the arena, where several other rookie cowboys were preparing to take their turns. There were waivers to sign and rules repeated. Adam had a hard time remaining focused on any of it because he could feel Faye's gaze on him from her position in the stands.

He really was the luckiest man alive. He'd finally found where he belonged. It wasn't a town or a city. It wasn't a specific job. It was knowing he had the love of a good woman and a future they could share together.

EPILOGUE

Four months later

Faye

The wind tousled Faye's hair as she stood at the edge of the clearing. She closed her eyes, breathed in deeply and allowed the smell of the Colorado hills to wash away all the turmoil she'd gone through several months ago.

Fall was setting in, and with every step she took, the smell of fallen leaves filled her senses. It had rained that morning, making everything appear clean and fresh. The sun would be setting soon. She only had a short amount of time up here before they'd need to head back.

Two strong arms wrapped around her waist, and Adam's chin rested on her shoulder. His low, warm voice made the hairs on the back of her neck lift and the churning in her stomach start up all over again.

"You're right," he said.

Faye chuckled. "I usually am. But what am I right about this time?"

He spun her around, his eyes piercing hers and that knowing grin on his face like he had a secret he didn't intend on sharing. "This place is amazing after the rain." Adam gestured toward the sky, lit in red, purple, and pink. The sky opened up around them, framed by the mountains and the tall trees of the valley below. "I get it now—why this place is one of your favorites."

She tilted her head, draping her arms around his neck." I don't know. I think your favorite spot is pretty nice too. Maybe after dinner we can take my mom's truck up on the lift."

Adam peered up at the sky overhead. "I'm not sure we'll get to see much. The sky is still pretty much covered from the storm clouds rolling out."

She grimaced. "You're probably right. Well, then we'll go tomorrow or the next day." She leaned into him, holding him tight. "As long as I'm with you, I'll be happy."

"I wanted to talk to you about that." There was an edge in his voice that wasn't there before, and it set off all kinds of warning bells in her head.

Was he going to try to join the rodeo again? No, it couldn't be that. Four months ago he'd participated in the bronc riding, and he'd done well and checked it off his bucket list. Afterward, though, when she'd asked him if he would ever do that again, he'd said no way. That it was exciting and terrifying all at once. But dating a daughter in the Zeke Callahan family fulfilled that role in his life. He didn't win the cash prize, but he'd won Faye's heart, and he said that was so much better.

Adam pulled away, grazing her jaw with his thumb. "You are the best thing to ever happen to me. I need you to know that."

"What's going on, Adam?"

He offered her a smile, but it did nothing to ease the tension that continued to grow in her gut. "I left Copper Creek in search of something. Then I left the city to come back, still trying to find my place—to find what's been missing in my life." Adam slowly dropped down onto one knee, and Faye gasped. He held her hand firmly in his. "I never dreamed the part of me that was missing was you."

One hand flew to her mouth. She'd figured they were on this path—to a future together—but she had no idea Adam had already gotten to this point in their relationship.

Still holding her left hand in his, he pulled out a ring from his pocket. He had it pinched between his finger and thumb and stared at it a moment before lifting his gaze to hers again.

"I love you more than anything. Wherever you are, I belong. Make me the happiest man alive and be mine forever."

The diamond was set in white gold and surrounded by other smaller stones. It wasn't large by any means, but that didn't matter. Just like the man who offered it to her, it was perfect. Her voice caught in her throat, and she wasn't able to voice all the emotions coursing through her body.

Adam had been her first real love. What they'd gone through was more than she would have ever expected, but she knew it was necessary to cement their relationship. Faye attempted to swallow down the lump in her throat, but it wouldn't budge. She nodded, her strangled voice betraying her.

"Yes! Yes, I'll marry you." She threw her arms around him, nearly knocking them both to the soggy earth.

Her lips crushed over his, stealing a kiss that sealed her promise to him. Adam rose, lifting both of them from their precarious position. Hands at her waist, he lifted her in the air then put her back on the ground and kissed her. Neither one of them had to speak. This kiss in this moment on this mountainside said everything their hearts wanted to. Like Adam, she'd found where she belonged.

FAYE AND ADAM stood at the doors to the latest addition of the country club, waiting for the hostess to seat them. Not only had Shane added on to the building itself, but he'd managed to create something that the locals had only seen in the city.

There was outdoor seating around the back of the building on a covered veranda, along with the restaurant seating inside. This wasn't just some country bumpkin restaurant. It was arguably the nicest eating establishment in town or just on the outside of town.

Faye exchanged an excited look with Adam. "I can't believe you got reservations on his opening night. I heard he was only going to serve a few high-brow people—investors and the like."

Adam wrapped his arm around her waist and kissed her temple. "I may have called in a favor when he needed a few pieces of equipment fixed."

"What do you mean you can't deliver until the twentieth? I need those steaks by next Friday." Shane stormed out of a hallway, a phone to his ear. "I paid for rush delivery. You know what that means, don't you?" His eyes snagged on Faye and Adam, and his angry expression smoothed before he turned away from them. "You let your supervisor know that if these steaks don't get here on the date that I requested, I'll be going with another supplier." He shut off his phone and faced the couple. "I'm sorry about that." His face broke into a smile. "How are you two doing this evening?"

The awkward tension in the air dissipated when Adam reached for Faye's hand and showcased the ring. "I'm the happiest man alive tonight, and we plan on celebrating."

Shane's smile widened. "Well, congratulations!" He clapped Adam on the back. "That's excellent news! Be sure to tell your server to give you our best bottle of champagne on the house."

Faye waved her hand dismissively. "Oh, you don't have to—"

"Cousin! Is that you?"

Shane stiffened, and the happy smile he wore completely disappeared. Faye could have sworn he muttered the word "no" under his breath, but she couldn't be certain. He turned toward the source of whoever was speaking.

Eloise was there, flanked on either side by a man and a woman. While the three of them approached, Faye glanced once more at Shane to find him smiling again. She must have imagined his discomfort.

"Marc, Madeline, what are you guys doing here in Colorado?"

Madeline lunged forward and gave him a hug, though he remained stiff as a board. "Didn't you get our calls?" She pulled back to look at him fully. "We tried contacting you several times. We're here to visit. We've missed you."

Shane's rigid form was the only indication he might not be the happiest to discover this information. He glanced from the strangers to Eloise, then briefly to Faye and Adam before settling on Madeline. "I got your messages... I just didn't think you'd actually come."

She nudged his shoulder with her fingertips. "You're so funny. You always had the best sense of humor out of all the cousins, right Marc?"

"Absolutely," Marc agreed. He moved forward to give

Shane an awkward-looking hug just as Madeline moved out of the way. "It's been a long time since you were in LA. We heard you took your inheritance and invested in becoming a cowboy." His snide tone ruffled Faye's feathers. Being a cowboy wasn't easy. And Shane had done so much more than that. Marc gestured around them. "When I heard about that, I never dreamed this is what they meant. Dude, this place is top-notch. I bet you're just raking in the money, huh?"

Shane's eyes narrowed. He opened his mouth then snapped it shut just as quickly when his gaze landed on Eloise.

She must have noticed his confusion. "Oh, I was on my way home when I saw them broken down on the side of the road. They said they knew you, and I offered to bring them here." Eloise glanced at Faye and then back to Shane. "But now that they're here safe and sound, I'll be getting on my way."

"Cullen, party of two?"

Adam held up a hand. "That's us."

Eloise gave them a little wave and headed for the door. Faye glanced over her shoulder as Adam moved her toward the restaurant. Shane looked absolutely infuriated. His face was red and his hands were clenched at his sides. She dug her elbow into Adam's side, eliciting a grunt from him. "I think something is up with that."

"With what? With your elbow being sharper than a crowbar?" He rubbed his side, shooting her a hurt look.

"No. With Shane and his cousins. Didn't that exchange seem... weird?"

Adam looked behind them then shook his head. "Nah. Family stuff can be a lot murkier than you might realize. Shane will be fine. Let's focus on what *we're* celebrating, alright? I can't wait to spend the evening with my fiancée."

She grinned, leaning into him. "The evening, and the rest of our lives."

~

Hello reader,

Did you enjoy Faye and Adam's love story? Then you won't want to miss what's next with the Callahans...

Eloise Callahan is starting to feel left behind as her sisters find love and move on. But when she rescues a handsome stranded motorist, she can't help wondering if her luck might finally be changing.

Shane Owens never expected to fall for the strong, kind-hearted cowgirl who helped him—but danger follows him wherever he goes. Keeping Eloise safe means keeping his secrets close... and his heart even closer.

Can Shane protect Eloise without breaking her heart? Or will love be the one risk he can't afford to take?

Don't miss the suspense, secrets, and sweet romance in *Catching a Cowgirl, Callahans of Copper Creek Book 6!*
Look for the paperback at **nataliedeanbooks.com** and other retailers.